LITERALLY DEAD

A PEPPER BROOKS COZY MYSTERY

ERYN SCOTT

KRISTOPHERSON PRESS

Copyright © 2017 by Eryn Scott

Published by Kristopherson Press

All rights reserved.

www.erynwrites.com

erynwrites@gmail.com

Facebook: @erynscottauthor

Sign up for my newsletter to hear about new releases and sales!

No part of this book may be reproduced in any form or by any electronic or mechanical means, including information storage and retrieval systems, without written permission from the author, except for the use of brief quotations in a book review.

Cover by Paper and Sage Designs

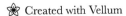 Created with Vellum

*For Mrs. Ferguson:
champion of literature, connoisseur of comedy, master of rebel lipstick shades.*

1

"To be an English major or not to be an English major? That is the question."

My Boston terrier barked as I recited my version of the first lines of Hamlet's soliloquy. I held her face as she panted up at me from the couch of my tiny college-apartment living room.

In addition to looking at my dog, I was looking at a metaphorical crossroads. And while mine had decidedly less bloody possible outcomes, it felt just as heavy as I'm sure Hamlet's had to him.

"Well? What do you think I should do?" I asked, staring into her brown eyes, waiting for—well, anything, really. I certainly didn't have a clear answer.

"You must be desperate if you're asking the dog." My roommate, Liv, walked into the room, rolling her eyes in my direction.

I sighed and flopped myself onto the couch next to the dog.

"Dogs have instincts about stuff like this. You never know. She might already know what my future holds."

"Ugh. You need to stop reading so much Shakespeare. It's making you dramatic and a little morbid," she said.

"What? Is not!"

"Pepper, in line at Bittersweet this morning, you said if someone took the last sesame bagel you might drown yourself in Campus Creek."

I pressed my lips together.

Liv continued. "And you said you were visited by the ghost of your old dog, Buttons, who told you to go to the pound, even though I saw the flyer for half-priced adoptions sitting on the counter last weekend."

Well, I had to give her those.

"Getting Hamburger was a great decision regardless of how it came to me."

Liv scoffed. "Yeah, the *many* talks we've had lately about you getting a dog must've had nothing to do with it, huh?" She raised her eyebrows as she watched me. "And you're seriously sticking with that name?"

I scooped Hamburger into my lap defensively and said, "I have to. Brooklyn picked it."

"I guess it's better the dog than the baby," Liv said.

Giggling at the memory, I nodded. I had stopped by my sister's house on the way home from the animal shelter that weekend. When I'd arrived, she and my niece, Brooklyn, were having a heated discussion—well, as heated as a discussion with a three-year-old can get—about how Brooklyn thought it her right as the older sister to name her new baby brother.

My sister had rested her hands on her eight-months-pregnant belly and sighed—a gesture for help if I'd ever seen one. So I told Brooklyn her mom and dad already had a name picked for her baby brother, but she could name my new dog instead. *Wasn't that more fun anyway?* The gratitude in my sister's tired eyes and the brightness in my niece's made the sacrifice well worth it.

"And when did you find out 'Hamburger' was the name Brooklyn was set on? Before or after your selfless act?"

I scrunched my nose slightly. "Erm—definitely after, but I feel like Hammy could be a nickname for Hamlet just as well as Hamburger."

Liv crossed the living room and scratched Hamburger's head. The dog snorted and wagged her bottom. Liv knelt down so she was face to face with Hammy.

"If naming a dog after a Shakespearian character doesn't convince your owner she's silly for doubting her major, I don't know what will."

She sent me a pointed look as she stood up. Envy shot through me as I watched her slick her long blond hair back into a tight power-ponytail, completing her awesome businesslady facade. If either of us was in the right major, it was her. She was so good at what she did—the guys in her business classes called her *the bull* because she never backed down—and she already had job offers rolling in for when we graduated next year.

Not only did she love the business world, it was a career that would all-but guarantee she would be living comfortably in a posh Seattle apartment within a year. Me? I was already strapped for cash, and a post-graduation life armed with only an English degree seemed even more bleak.

"Besides," Liv turned back toward me, "English is in your blood."

My eyes dropped to the floor, along with my stomach. It had almost been a year since my father had died, but talking about him still made me cringe with pain as much as it had the day I'd learned about his heart attack. He had been an English professor here at Northern Washington University and everyone had always assumed I would follow in his footsteps.

"Yeah, that's part of the problem," I said under my breath.

Liv muttered in complaint at my statement, knowing my theory about how the only reason I'd chosen my major was because I was still mourning the loss of my father. But I maintain I'd been fragile, deciding with my heart instead of my mind.

Honestly, I would've changed majors months ago if it hadn't been for Dr. Ferguson, my mentor. Aside from being one of the coolest ladies I'd ever met, Sharon Ferguson was a brilliant professor who made you believe literature could change the world. The only issue was as world changing as literature could be, I was beginning to doubt its pocket-filling, bacon-bringing abilities.

Liv headed for the door. "Hey, I've gotta go, but let's continue this never-ending conversation after I have my mock interview class and you go to that lecture thing, K?"

I scoffed, put Hammy on the couch, and then stood up. "Lecture *thing*? How dare you reduce my—"

She waved her hand toward me. "Okay, okay. Your big-shot-from-Oxford lecture thing."

"How'd you know he's from Oxford?" I asked, sure I hadn't mentioned it to her.

"You're not the only English nerd I know." She winked at me. "My friend, Gina, is in Evilsworth's American Lit. this quarter," Liv said, using my nickname for my most hated professor of all time. Professor Evensworth's mission in life was to break young, hopeful students until they realized they would never be as knowledgeable as him. He taught American Literature exclusively, as he claimed everything else was crap.

"Gina said Evilsworth spent a whole period ripping on this Dr. Campbell, and how he'd wasted his career studying Shakespeare," Liv continued. "He told them to skip the lecture at first, but changed his mind by the end of class and decided to give them extra credit if they could write up a detailed essay outlining the flaws in his logic." She shot me a pointed look. "You English people are so intense."

I rolled my eyes. He hadn't said anything of the sort during our class yesterday, but I wouldn't put it past him. "Evilsworth is just jealous. Dr. Campbell's going to be great. Did you know he and Fergie were university mates at Oxford?" I let my eyes slip to my watch. "Speaking of the lecture, I've got to go help Fergie get everything set up. I'll walk with you to campus."

I gave Hammy one last pat on the head. She plopped herself into a heap on top of her chewy bone.

The air was crisp and wonderful as we stepped outside and headed down the street toward NWU. It was a surprisingly sunny evening for fall, but the sun was already setting and I knew it would be dark in a matter of hours.

I looked around at the streets I'd known since I was a little girl, when my dreams of college were limited to wearing small NWU sweatshirts and riding my bike past the tall, stately buildings. Growing up in a university town had been quite the dichotomy. During the school year, the town was bustling with students, but during the summer, when the majority of them went back to their homes, our town took a deep breath and closed its eyes in the silence, if only for a few months. It was during those summers when it felt like the town grew closer. There was an intense bonding when you were part of the "townies."

My gaze traveled down the street to my favorite second-hand clothing shop. I'd always been a thrifty shopper, never quite growing out of one of my rebellious teenage phases. I'd done my best to separate myself from my parents' wealth and success, but lately my frugal ways had been coming in handy.

Liv craned her neck and said, "Looks like there's a new rack outside." Her blue eyes sparkled as she turned to me. "Do you think they're having a sale?"

Meeting Liv had only fueled my thrift-shopping habit. She was a pro at getting the best deals to add to her you-wouldn't-know-it-was-second-hand wardrobe. I'd taken her into Second Pantses her first week in town and she'd been in love.

"Ugh. I can't look." I averted my eyes to the sidewalk in front of us. "It's too tempting. The only reason I should be setting foot in that store is to bring in a box for consignment."

Liv grunted. "Or you could ask your mom for money."

I pointed a finger at her and narrowed my eyes. "Don't you even. She understands my need to pay for as much as I can, said she admires it, even." I didn't add how my mom being away on a two-week trip to the east coast also had a little to do with it. I wasn't about to interrupt her business trip with my money problems.

"Well as long as it works for both of you," Liv said, shaking her head. Her dad was some big-shot banking guy in Seattle and she'd gladly accepted his money when he wanted to fully support her in school.

Because my dad had worked at the university, I'd gotten a pretty big tuition break already, so it was the least I could do to pay for the rest myself. Growing up with a prominent professor as a dad and my mom, a powerful lawyer—not to mention an appointee to the university board of regents twice in a row—had its perks. After twenty-one years, however, I couldn't tell you what I'd actually accomplished on my own and what had happened because of my family. I was an adult now and I wanted to see what I could do without my family's influence. Hence the selling of my stuff to pay for my living expenses and college.

While Liv didn't seem to share my qualms about taking family money, she had her own family baggage. Her dad treated her like the son he never had—even going so far as to try to slip the name Oliver on her birth certificate, instead of Olivia—so I didn't take her teasing too personally, knowing I wasn't the only one with weird family hang-ups.

We maneuvered our way through a steady stream of other university students who were undoubtedly heading toward the student center for dinner.

"See you later," I said as the business building came into view.

Liv waved and then disappeared inside. I kept going further into campus. The walkways buzzed with students, but besides waving at a few familiar faces, I didn't stop to talk or lounge on the grass. I was cutting it pretty close if I wanted to help Fergie before the lecture.

Passing by my favorite garden in the center of campus, a shiver raced up my spine as I watched someone break off from the crowd near the student center and walk in my direction. Nathan Newton, or Naked Newt, as my sister and her friends always called him in high school—because of his propensity for streaking and his slightly sticky-looking skin texture—was by far the creepiest guy in Pine Crest.

I skirted closer to the English building.

Now, don't get me wrong. I have nothing against odd people. Heck, I was one of them myself. I mean, I had spent most of childhood convinced I was Nancy Drew's auburn haired sister, and definitely should've been her sidekick instead of stupid Bess. I seriously even carried around a magnifying glass for the better part of three years. So unusual, I got.

Naked Newt was a different story. He was something like eleven feet tall, looked liked a washed-out, old oil painting of a frustrated British general, and his pale lips were always pursed as if he were holding an invisible toothpick between them.

He had a penchant for wording everything in a way which would make even Edgar Allen Poe's skin crawl. His brown irises were so dark, he appeared to have black eyes. The way he stared people down made you feel like he was trying to steal your soul.

My stomach churned as I watched Newt turn onto the path that would meet up with the one I was on.

Why was he even on campus anyway? Newt didn't go to school at NWU. Sure, he still lived with his odd grandma, Louise, but their house was on the other side of town.

I pulled my face into what I hoped was a smile, but was probably more like a grimace, as Newt approached.

"Good evening, Pepper," he said in that weird tone of his. He'd always had a slight British accent, even though he'd spent his whole life here in Washington and his grandma was like, Romanian or something.

"Hey, New—er—Nate."

"The air has a lovely iron quality this evening, does it not?" His nostrils flared and his lips pursed even tighter, making the lines deepen in the moist-looking skin around his mouth. "Like a hint of blood riding on the breeze."

I frowned. Iron? Blood? Seriously? And Liv thought *I* was being morbid. I suppressed a full-body shudder and faked a laugh. "Haha! Totally!" Then I skirted past him and fast-walked the rest of the way to the English building.

But even as the heavy glass doors closed behind me, I could feel his dark eyes watching me.

2

"Gross, gross, gross." I rounded the corner into the first hallway and then danced about for a minute to get rid of the shivers.

Closing my eyes, I breathed in slow and steady, taking comfort in the familiar smell of the old building. The dusty smell of classic books permeated the halls.

That smell was my father. It was my childhood spent reading in the mustard-colored armchair which sat in the corner of his office, the spiky ferns ticking my feet as they hung over the arm rest. And based on my current major, that smell was my future.

The smile pulling across my face belied another reason I had yet to change my major. When I was here, studying literature, talking to my peers and professors, in the thick of it, I loved it. Only when I strayed from the English building did the fears about my future begin to crop up and multiply.

My pulse relaxed. There may not be a whole lot of money in English, but there sure was an abundance of nostalgia.

Checking my watch, I realized how late I was running. I

made my way back into the main foyer and took the corner toward the lecture hall at a bit of a reckless pace.

"Ooof! Oh dear!" The shrill, overly dramatized voice of Dr. Ferguson rang out as I smashed into her.

My arms flailed as I tried to find the wall to steady myself.

"Omigosh, I'm so sorry, Fergie!" I said as I finally untangled myself from my professor and readjusted my messenger bag.

"Pepper, what on earth is the great rush?" Her voice rose with each word and she swiped her hair back into place. Dr. Ferguson's wispy gray hair did little to cover her scalp, even in the combover she always fashioned it into.

"Sorry, I was on my way to help you. You needed some students to show up early, right?"

It was only then I realized she wasn't alone. A frail young woman stepped out from behind my teacher.

Dr. Ferguson straightened and pushed her shoulders back. "Oh, well—yes—as a matter of fact, yes I do. Thank you, Pepper."

From the redness splotching her cheeks to the shiftiness in her eyes, Fergie seemed downright flustered. This wasn't a regular look for her. Sure, the woman was disorganized and dramatic, but she was a literary genius, a leader in a profession built by old white men created to celebrate other old white men's writing.

"What can I help with?" I asked.

"Yes, well—" She pressed her bright red lips together—the woman often applied her lipstick so liberally it ventured over her lip line in wobbly patches. "I'm taking Stephanie, here…" Fergie glanced behind her, then spun around to locate the small woman as if she were a toddler she couldn't seem to keep in her sights.

And while only slightly bigger than a child, the willowy woman looked to be in her late twenties or early thirties. Her blond hair was pulled back into a smart, low bun and her eyes were the lightest shade of blue I'd ever seen, blinking back at me from behind long mascara-free lashes. A blue, cotton button-up shirt hung off her diminutive shoulders, almost down to her black-legging-clad knees, but I had a sneaking suspicion on anyone normal-sized, it would hit just below the waist.

"Oh Stephanie! Good, there you are!" Fergie said, halting in her spin then looking back to me. "Pepper, this is Dr. Campbell's daughter, Stephanie."

"Stepdaughter." The words came out in a soft British-accented monotone. Other than the slight movement her light pink lips made, I wouldn't have been able to tell they came from her. She smiled, seemingly embarrassed.

I held my hand out to shake hers. It was soft and delicate as if she had the bones of a robin. I pulled away after a soft squeeze and watched her hand flutter back by her side.

"Right, right, stepdaughter. Stephanie accompanied Dr. Campbell from Britain to consult with our biology department on a few plant-y things." Fergie nodded toward Stephanie who appeared simultaneously unnerved at Dr. Ferguson's wording and also as if a strong gust of wind might push her right over.

"That's great…" I didn't know what else to say. "Too bad you'll miss his lecture, though."

Stephanie shook her head. "He practices them with me. I've already heard it many times." At this, a little emotion rang in her voice and it didn't seem so monotone anymore.

She was his travel buddy. I remember being Dad's when he would go to guest lecture. He always said I was the best company, a good luck charm for a successful performance.

"Oh, good. So you're going to talk plants, then?" I asked because asking such an obvious question seemed like a better option than bursting into tears about my dead dad.

"I'm a botanist and I'm always interested in meeting with my peers in other countries."

"Yes, yes. Simply the *most* interesting." Fergie caught my arm in her long bony grasp and she widened her blue-eye-shadowed eyes in warning. We didn't have time to stand around and chat, and I should've known better. "Would you be a dear and go check on our esteemed guest speaker? Make sure he's ready," she said, letting my arm go. Without even waiting for my answer, she patted my cheek. "I'm quite sure he'll be in my office. Thanks." Then she spun around and headed toward the front entrance, Stephanie trailing behind her. "You're a doll, Pepper," Fergie said loudly over her shoulder.

I chuckled. Between her high operatic voice, the silky draped clothing she was always flipping this way and that, and her interesting pear-shaped body, Fergie was a force of nature. She was closing in on seventy, yet still managed to teach four sections of beginning to high-level English as well as volunteering as a "stage hand"—which really just meant she spent her time bossing around the actual director—for the theater department's production each semester.

After this, her most recent dramatic retreat, I blinked, laughing again at the woman's eccentric ways and turned in the direction that would lead me to the lecture hall and her office. It was then excited butterflies began to flutter in my stomach.

I was about to meet the famous Dr. Campbell.

We'd been studying his latest paper on Hamlet, which outlined his somewhat controversial take on the true identity of the ghost—he argued the ghost was more of a projection of young Hamlet than his dead father come back to haunt him. While I found his logic sound and his argument interesting, the truth was I was mostly intrigued with him because of how highly Fergie spoke of him.

I turned and walked down the hallway where many of the professors' offices were located. There were four in a cluster here with a small kitchen and lounge area for them to relax between classes or to meet with students.

Walking into the room, my eyes instinctively went to the door on the very right, Dad's old office. Up until last fall, the first thing I would've done would've been to peek into the small side window and see if he was in. If he was, I would plop down into that mustard-colored chair—the one which now sat in the corner of my small bedroom back in the apartment—and we would chat about our days or debate something one of my professors had said in class. If he wasn't in, I would leave a quick note, sometimes borrowing a book to read even though my stack of things to get through for class was becoming more like a tower on my desk.

My throat felt hot and dry as I stood there now, still somehow stunned at the fact he was gone. It helped that Dr. Ferguson's office was in the same cluster. The months following Dad's death, I had walked in there a few times, either because I'd forgotten he was really gone or because I needed to see something that reminded me of him.

It was then Fergie and I had gotten so close. She would either come wrap her arm around me and usher me into her office for tea and conversation, or I would take a few steps left and knock on her door instead of his, making up some question I had about class. If the woman saw through my facade—which she probably did, she was as sharp as Katherine's tongue in *Taming of the Shrew*—she never let on.

Over the months, my feet had stopped taking me to his door, heading toward Fergie's instead, which I did today, with only a slight sigh.

The blinds were pulled closed in the little window to her office, so I couldn't see inside. Dr. Campbell was a bit of a celebrity around here, if you were anyone but Evilsworth, so I'm sure she was trying to keep his location quiet to give him a little breathing room before the lecture.

I knocked on the door and waited.

Even leaning close so my ear was almost pressed up to the dark wooden door, I couldn't hear a thing. Had Fergie told him not to answer if someone knocked?

After a moment, I decided to go in anyway. I mean, she'd told me to go check on him. They couldn't get mad at me when I had orders from a professor, right?

I nodded in a hopeful answer to my question and clasped the door handle, pushing it down until it clicked open.

"Hello," I said in a singsong voice. As I pushed the door open even more, I caught sight of Dr. Campbell sitting behind Fergie's desk. His back was to me, but I could tell he was slumped forward, head resting on his forearm looking away from me.

I almost giggled, but caught myself, suddenly regretting my loud hello. The guy was fast asleep.

Glancing at the clock on the wall, however, I couldn't get past how close we were to his lecture time. He really needed to start getting prepped. I walked closer and gently patted his shoulder as I said, "Dr. Campbell, sir. It's time to get up."

His body shook with my touch, but he didn't wake. I scooted behind him and walked around his other side,

Literally Dead

where I could get in his face like Dad always had to do when I wouldn't wake up for junior high.

"Dr. Campbell. It's time to wake up for your lecture, I'm Pepper Brooks, Dr. Ferguson's student and she sent me he—" My voice cut out as his face came into view and his open eyes made me jump in surprise as I let out a high-pitched squeak.

"Oh!" I giggled nervously. "Hahaha! Whew. You got me there! Very funny, pretending to be asleep."

My face was hot and I was wishing I hadn't squeaked. I wasn't one of those girls who couldn't handle surprises; I was Nancy Drew's long lost sister, tough and just the person you'd want by your side when you were solving a mystery. Definitely *not* a squeaker.

But as I watched him, Dr. Campbell didn't seem to be judging me for the squeak. Actually, he didn't seem to be doing anything—not laughing, not sitting up, not blinking... not even breathing.

Come to think of it, there was a ghostly pallor to his skin.

Holy crap, holy crap. I backed away. I tried to swallow, but my throat was bone dry.

No. This wasn't happening. Dr. C was just one of those rare people who slept incredibly soundly... with their eyes open. Finally gathering enough saliva to swallow, I stepped forward once more, jostling his shoulder with more force.

"Dr. Campbell. Wake up," I almost yelled, adding a quiet, "dammit, man" to the end. A heat settled in my throat and my mouth tasted like pennies.

More vigorous shaking did seem to elicit movement, but it was the heavy sliding of a lifeless heap. I leaned forward, putting two fingers against his wrist. There was no pulse. And then there was the open prescription bottle lying on its side next to his left hand, with a few little white pills spilling out onto the desk.

The room tipped. I threw my hand out to help support myself as I swayed. In doing so, I accidentally knocked his hand aside, enough that I could see a piece of paper was trapped under his right hand, scrawled writing covering half of it.

I had already moved him, so it wouldn't be a big deal if I scooted his hand a few inches to read what he had been writing, right?

With my thumb and pointer finger, I delicately picked up the appendage and moved it to the side. His skin was not cold, necessarily, but definitely not the recommended ninety-eight point six degrees. A shiver ran down my spine. I tried to focus on the words on the page instead of that realization.

Maybe it was because I'd been staring at those very words for the last week, trying my hand at memorizing the soliloquy, but they jumped out at me, making me lean in to make sure I was right.

On the paper, he had written the first part of Hamlet's soliloquy, the pen still stuck in his lifeless hand.

To be, or not to be: that is the question:
Whether 'tis nobler in the mind to suffer
The slings and arrows of outrageous fortune,
Or to take arms against a sea of troubles,
And by opposing end them? To die: to sleep;
No more; and by a sleep to say we end
The heart-ache, and the thousand natural shocks
That flesh is heir to, 'tis a consummation
Devoutly to be wish'd. To die, to sleep;
To sleep: perchance to dream: ay, there's the rub;
For in that sleep of death what dreams might come
When we have shuffled

While the handwriting started out neat, it deteriorated decidedly as it went. By the last few lines, there was a rushed slant to it. The last line wasn't even finished, but the rest of it, plus the next few lines, rattled off in my brain without effort.

I blinked and backed away, heart hammering in my ears, the room tipping.

I needed to get help. I needed to tell someone right away. I ran out into the cluster, but found it empty, so I kept going into the hall.

"Help!" I yelled, seeing a group of people gathering by the lecture hall. "Help! Someone needs to call 911!" I ran toward them, all but forgetting my cellphone was sitting in my messenger bag, which hung on my shoulder.

I think I was starting to understand Bess a little better.

3

I stumbled upon a cluster of startled students first. Each of them held a phone, about to head into the lecture and catching up on social media before being forced to part from the device for the duration.

Unfortunately, they held no better emergency instincts than I, and remained frozen for a moment as I tumbled into the wall and gasped for breath.

"9... 1...1..." I panted, hoping the weird taste in my mouth was merely my body's reaction to running for the first time in years and not a sign I was going to throw up.

"What happened?" a girl with glasses asked.

I physically felt my face drain of color like a cartoon character who's just seen a ghost. It's a thing, I know that now; I felt it happen, felt the heat leave my skin like the water level in a bathtub unplugged.

"Campbell... he's... ambulance." The words tripped out of me, spilling and flopping end over end, in all the wrong order.

The next few seconds felt like minutes, hours. They stretched in front of me like a slinky, tunneling and telescoping. I watched glasses-girl poke the screen of her phone, then hold it up to her ear. I could hear the others ask me questions, but I couldn't concentrate on anything but that phone.

Then, the girl's eyes met mine and it was like I could read her mind. *What should I tell them?* she thought at me.

"I think he's dead. He's in Professor Ferguson's office." My words sent shivers down every surface of skin I possessed. Or maybe that was the effect of watching all four people in the group stiffen and blink unbelievingly at my statement.

Once glasses-girl hung up her phone, the building erupted into a cacophony of movement and noise.

Despite my slight lapse in judgment, my Drew-sister's instincts were coming back to me, and I headed back to the office, standing guard so no one would accidentally stumble onto the body or sneak inside for a peek and possibly tamper with evidence—er, well—no more than I already had.

When the paramedics arrived, I was pushed aside and everything whirled around me.

"Pepper?" An EMT rushed toward me where I'd planted myself on one of the couches in the middle of the lounge.

I looked up into the dark eyes of my high school friend, Fiona, who'd gone on to become an EMT.

"Oh, hey Fi," I mumbled.

She set down her stuff and squatted in front of me, checking my eyes and holding my wrist while she eyed her watch.

"Are you okay? You found the body?" Her face squinted in concern and I flinched as she said those two words, but nodded, nonetheless, hoping it would do to answer both of Fi's questions.

Literally Dead

"How's Pepper doing, Fiona?" I recognized the voice of our local fire chief. He poked his head out from the office and gave me a short wave and a sympathetic look before focusing back on Fi.

"She's okay. Slightly shaken, but okay," Fiona called over her shoulder. "I got her."

Police showed up a few minutes later, sending their own waves and sympathetic looks toward me as they combed the place, asked a bunch of questions, and put up tape to keep people where they wanted them.

Then Dr. Ferguson appeared at the doorway of the lounge, her face a mixture of ghostly white and flushed worry.

"What in heaven's name is going on here?"

It felt like I was watching an operatic entrance, her voice getting louder and higher in tone as the question unfolded from her dramatic form.

Pine Crest's largest cop, Frank Fitz, intimidating despite his red bulbous nose and the few-too-many pounds he stored around his waist, stepped toward Fergie, his hand held up in a "hold on, ma'am" kind of way. But she slapped it away and tried to side step past the big man. He was faster though, and moved to block her, grabbing her arms gently when she reached up to push him.

"Davis? Oh, Davis!" She sobbed as her eyes landed on the body, visible through the open door to her office. Her body began to sag in Frank's grip and finally crumpled to the floor.

During her display of emotion, I was reminded she and Dr. Campbell had been old school mates and this wasn't Fergie being dramatic; she had been close to the man. The sadness in her eyes made me look away and shuffle my feet on the gray carpet.

Until I heard, "And Pepper!"

I glanced up just in time to see a blur of flowy fabrics, red lips, and bright-blue eye shadow headed in my direction. She enveloped me in a tight, sobbing hug.

"I'm so sorry. Did you find him like this? You must be terrified, my poor girl." Fergie squeezed me tight, but I got the feeling the hug was more for her than me, so I tightened my arms and patted her back, too.

She finally pulled away, her face streaked with black mascara, red lipstick smeared.

I shook my head, feeling teary as I met her pained eyes. "I thought he was taking a nap, like some sort of before-lecture ritual." I swallowed, trying not to relive the whole thing. "What happened?"

She sat up straight. "What *did* happen?" Her voice rose along with her body and by the end of the question, she was standing, looking around her with a pleading expression on her smeared face.

A man stepped forward. He was not one of the policemen I knew or Pine Crest's head inspector, who I expected to be running the investigation. This man was around six feet tall and looked a lot like he'd stepped out of an old movie with his long, camel-colored duster, slicked-back dark hair, substantial eyebrows, and "frankly, darling, I don't give a damn" expression.

"Hi there, ma'am. I'm Detective Valdez." He had a voice as smooth as an Italian leather-bound classic, only I think the hint of accent I heard was more Latin-American than Italian. The man held out his tanned hand and Dr. Ferguson shook it suspiciously. "This is your office?" he asked, looking at Fergie. "And you found the body?" He turned his gaze toward me.

I could see Fergie flinch at the word "body," but she and

I began nodding at the same time in the same slow, this-is-surreal way.

"I have a few more things to finish up, but then can I ask you some questions?"

Since we were still nodding, we kept doing so until he left. Then Fergie grabbed hold of my hands and squeezed them tightly as she met my eyes, hers full of questions.

"His note," I started, but stopped to swallow the metallic taste gathering in my mouth. "It was Hamlet's soliloquy."

Her drawn-on eyebrows scrunched together. "To be, or not to be..." she whispered, the last *be* trailing off. She shook her head. "Oh, my dear Davis. What have you done?" The old woman's eyes closed tightly and more mascara-stained tears slid down her cheeks.

I knew she was jumping to the same conclusion I'd come to after seeing the words of such a tortured character next to the slumped-over figure of Dr. Campbell.

There's been much debate throughout the years about the true meaning behind the "To be or not to be" soliloquy—I should know. I had to read close to a dozen different arguments for a paper last semester. Some scholars think the character is simply wondering why any of us are here. What is life? Others believe Hamlet is considering taking revenge for the murder of his father and worries such a fight may lead to his death. But probably the most widely held belief is Hamlet is severely depressed because of his father's death and his mother marrying his uncle—none other than the killer himself—and is considering suicide.

To be, or not to be. To live or to take one's life. Chilling a thought as it was, it would make sense for such a Shakespearian-focused mind to leave a soliloquy instead of the usual list of goodbyes tangled up with reasons. From what

Dr. Ferguson told us in preparation for his visit, Dr. Campbell ate, drank, slept—and apparently, died—The Bard.

"I'm so sorry," I said to Fergie.

She swiped at her teary face. "His wife, Stephanie's mom, passed away this year and he was terribly sad, but I never thought..." she trailed off, shaking her head.

Suddenly, the older woman's fingers clamped down on mine and her eyes snapped open.

"Stephanie." The name was a gasp. "And the lecture. Someone must tell the students." She used her free hand to snap at the rotund policeman.

Based on the way Frank's eyebrows rose and his jaw clenched tight, he either hadn't forgotten the slapping or was simply adding this to her rap sheet of mild offenses.

"Yeah?" he asked as he stepped closer, hooking his thumbs into his police pants pockets.

"Sir, we *desperately* need someone to go inform the crowd—which has no doubt formed in the lecture hall—that tonight's talk is cancelled." Her words were loud and she paused in all the most dramatic places. Each syllable of "desperately" felt like its own word and when she said, "cancelled," her voice seemed to crumble, becoming a new sob and her shoulders shook as she let her head hang.

I sent a pleading look at Frank. "His stepdaughter is here, at the university, too. She's in the botany department. I think someone should inform her..."

I paused, remembering when I'd been pulled out of class with the news Dad had collapsed at home, was in the hospital, how it didn't look good.

Blinking away the memory, I finished with, "Her name is Stephanie." A sigh settled on my chest, knowing all too well what the poor girl was about to go through.

Fortunately, Frank's annoyed jaw unclenched and his

eyes softened, then he nodded and jotted down the information about where to find Stephanie and what to tell those gathering by the lecture hall before heading out of the room.

Dr. Ferguson still clutched my right hand, but she'd sat up, no longer letting her head hang near her lap. She was watching people bustle about. Her eyes held a blank expression and she seemed utterly out of words, I think a first for this loud, drama-loving lady.

Not sure there was anything better I could do for her other than continue to hold her hand, I used my left hand to fish my phone out of my bag. I didn't know how long this was going to take, but I didn't want to take any chances when Hamburger was still learning our house routine. She wasn't a puppy, but I'd only had her for a few days and I didn't want to leave her for too long.

So I texted Liv.

"Hey. So I'm going to be out later than I thought. Will you make it home in time to let Hammy out? Long story, but I'm going to have to answer questions for the police. Dr. Campbell is dead."

I licked my lips and set my phone in my lap. Everything felt surreal, especially having to type that last sentence. Liv was probably right in the middle of her mock interview, so I hoped her phone was on silent. It usually was. Both Liv and I had been scolded during our freshman year for forgetting to silence our phones, so we just kept them on vibrate all the time now. My phone buzzed in my lap as a text came through. That was fast.

"OMG. Like literally dead?!"

My fingers hovered over the screen or a moment before typing a response.

"Literally. Dead. No figurative about it. I found him. Looks like he pulled a 'to be, or not to be.'"

The bubble popped up on my screen, showing Liv was writing back.

"He fell off the stage?"

I chuckled, which felt good after so much sadness, but I also didn't want to seem insensitive to those around me, so I kept it to a mild snort. Plus, what I had to write in response pushed all happy thoughts aside.

"No. He committed suicide."

My skin washed hot and cold as I typed the words. At first, I thought I'd opted for the Hamlet reference simply to avoid having to type them, but the more I thought about it, the more I realized something didn't quite feel right. My phone buzzed, pulling me back.

"Oh…okay. I'll let Hammy out. Almost done here, actually. Let me know if I can help. Be safe."

Despite the nagging feeling in the back of my mind, I smiled at Liv's worry for me and slid my phone back into my bag, taking a chance to look around now that things seemed to be calming down.

Detective Valdez emerged from the office and looked straight at me. I wasn't sure the man ever showed much emotion on his face, but his tight posture led me to believe he was thinking hard as he sat on the worn couch across from Fergie and myself.

He pulled out a notepad and said, "Alright. Ready to tell me what happened?"

"I told the paramedics everything when they got here."

He nodded. "I know. We want to make sure everything matches up, that there's nothing you missed telling us right after the trauma of finding him."

Inwardly, I rolled my eyes. Asking witnesses to repeat their stories multiple times was common practice. *Duh*, I scolded myself. *I should've known that.*

Fergie came to during the scolding I was giving myself and she let go of my hand. When I glanced over at her, she was nodding.

"Yes, dear. Tell it again. They need to do these things."

Taking a deep breath, I told the detective everything. Finding Dr. Campbell, touching his shoulder, seeing his open eyes, shaking him, searching for a pulse, then running to find help. At any mention of touching the body, the detective's eyes would narrow in a flinching way for just a second.

"Sorry. I should've known better than to touch him—anything, for that matter. He definitely slid when I shook him. And then I moved his hand so I could read the note." My heart was beating fast all over again as I recounted my actions.

At that last part, Detective Valdez's eyes closed for a whole second. "What?" he asked, his accent becoming more pronounced.

My eyes shifted between him, Fergie, and the few people who stopped at his raised question. "Um... I shook him?"

The detective put his pen down. "Is that a question Miss Brooks?"

I shook my head. "No. I shook him... to see if he was sleeping. And I moved his hand. I'm so sorry." I could picture Nancy Drew tsking at me and Bess tipping her head in a "told you it was tough" kinda way.

"Well, lucky for you, Miss Brooks, this seems to be a pretty cut and dry case."

Fergie breathed the question, "Suicide?" next to me.

The detective only dipped his head once as an answer, but it was enough. "Please stay close in the next few days as we may have more questions for the two of you."

We agreed to do so and he walked to the side of the

room to talk with one of the police officers. Which was when Stephanie spun into the lounge, eyes wide and frantic.

My heart stabbed with memories and I had to look away, almost wanted to cover my ears.

"Where is he?" Her fingers clutched the doorframe.

A police officer pointed her toward the office, his face grim.

Dr. Ferguson patted my knee. "You head home, Pepper. I'll sit with Stephanie."

I nodded without a fight, glad to be released even though I felt guilty for the sense of relief thinking of leaving gave me. Not needing to grab anything, my messenger bag still slung across my shoulder, I left, winding through the halls on autopilot until I was able to swing open an exterior door and take a full breath. It was dark outside and people were everywhere, crowded as close as they could get around the police barriers. Their faces were all a blur, their voices murmurs as I sped past them.

Taking none of my usual time to smell the smoky, fall nighttime air or saunter over the pathways, I arrived home in record time.

Hammy barked and ran to the door as I closed it behind me. Instinctively, I put my keys on the hook by the door and pulled my bag off my shoulders, dumping it onto the floor as I knelt down to pet the little black and white dog.

Liv came out of her room, her forehead creased as her dark brown eyes met mine. Without a word, she came over and pulled me into a hug.

I wasn't normally a crier, but ever since my dad passed away, the reaction was—inconveniently—happening more often. Luckily, I kept it to a few drops running down my cheek before I was able to compose myself.

Liv pulled back. "I can't believe it." She shook her head

and sat down on the couch. "Tell me absolutely everything. I mean, if you're not sick of talking about it, that is."

"No, it's okay."

So I told her everything I'd told the solemn Detective Valdez.

"Taking your own life." Her voice was a mere whisper as her eyes searched off somewhere past the white walls of our apartment.

I tried to breathe easier. I was at home, I was safe, Hamburger was crashed out in my lap, snoring up a storm. But there was something bugging me about the whole thing. I couldn't quite put my finger on it.

That night, I had a hard time getting to sleep. I kept replaying the night over and over in my mind. But it wasn't because I was scared or scarred even. My brain couldn't seem to let go of something.

Finally, my eyelids closed, heavy after the day's intensities. Hammy snored at the foot of the bed as I drifted into a fitful sleep, something lurking in the back of my unconscious thoughts.

4

"Might!" I yelled, sitting up in my bed the next morning.

Hamburger barked and jumped up, her short legs flailing as she tried to find her footing in the sea of comforter. Her eyes moved about the room, wild for a moment before they landed on me.

"It said *might*, Hammy. That's what was bothering me!" I blinked the sleep out of my eyes and pawed at my hair.

There was a knock at the door and Liv opened it, peeking inside. "You two okay in here?"

Hammy barked again.

Liv's face was red and sweaty, her blond hair pulled into a high ponytail. She was the kind of disciplined person who got up earlier than she actually had to so she could "fit in a workout." She usually started every morning with a yoga video and then went to the gym later if she could. Businesslady pants didn't seem as forgiving as leggings, however, so I didn't blame her.

Being a legging person—unable to ever see myself wearing one of the power pantsuits Liv would have to don daily when she got a job—I was less of a workout kind of person and more of an "eat salad for two days to make up for the three scones I gobbled up while I was at the coffee house reading" person. Gyms weren't my thing. Mornings weren't really my thing, either.

But my eyes were wide and I felt very awake that particular morning, because I had finally figured out what had been bothering me about the whole terrible Dr. Campbell situation last night.

"Liv, the soliloquy uses the word 'may,' but on the note Dr. Campbell left behind, he'd written 'might'." I shook my head; I should've caught it sooner. "It's actually, 'What dreams *may* come'."

My roommate pressed her lips together and lifted her eyebrows in an I'm-humoring-a-crazy-person way. "Okay… cool?" She wiped her sweaty forehead.

"He was a Shakespearean studies professor. He would be the last person to get that word wrong." I chewed on my lip. "And why was his writing so rushed?" I looked to Liv as if she might have the answer. "Aren't suicides usually planned out? Why would his handwriting be so sloppy toward the end? He didn't even finish the line he was on. This doesn't feel right."

Liv, understanding more of what I was talking about now, leaned into the doorframe, losing the confused expression. "The man was probably in a bad space, Pepper. I'm sure he made a mistake. Maybe he thought he would have more time before…" She trailed off and glanced down at her bare feet.

"I suppose." I scratched at an itch on my nose. "It's just, you know how you always say 'you English people are so weird'?" Liv nodded. "We *are*, especially about stuff like this. If he was going to go through the trouble to off himself to the tune of Hamlet's most sulky soliloquy, a true lifelong fan of The Bard wouldn't do it halfway. Shakespeare plays are full of drama and death and betrayal and more drama."

"Well, are you sure it's 'may'? I mean, like you said, the guy was an expert. Is it possible he knows of some old, original version where it said 'might' instead?"

My mouth dropped open and I pulled in a quick breath. "Oh my gosh. What if I *am* wrong? Oh no. We finished reading Hamlet last semester and I returned my copy to the library, so I've been using the internet to practice the soliloquy. What if I've been looking at an incorrect version?" I flipped the covers off my legs and jumped out of bed.

"Where are you going?" she asked, as I ran into the Jack and Jill bathroom between our bedrooms. Hamburger ran around my feet, excited by the movement.

"To the only place that matters in times like these!" I yelled dramatically as I splashed water on my face. "To the library!" Hamburger barked—probably only because I was yelling, but I pretended she was cheering me on.

I could almost feel Liv's eye roll through the wall. I didn't care; I had to figure this out.

"Yeah, and I'm sure your impending visit to the library has nothing to do with a dark-haired someone who happens to work in the mornings," Liv said as she turned her yoga video back on.

Scrunching my nose, I decided to pretend I hadn't heard that part.

MINUTES LATER, my teeth and hair were both brushed, I'd pulled on some skinny jeans and an oatmeal-colored sweater, and then I finished the whole thing off by pulling my hair into a bun and twisting a scarf around my neck.

Liv told me she would take Hammy on her morning walk, so I grabbed my bag and then pulled it over my head and onto one shoulder. It was a chilly gray day outside and wasn't raining as much as misting, the tiny bits of water seemed to hang stagnant in the air instead of dropping. By the time I crossed the street, the little droplets coated my sweater, my hair, and stuck to my eyelashes.

This was fall in Washington and I loved it. I pulled my sweater tighter and headed toward the Gretta Rosario Memorial Library. My stomach flipped excitedly as I closed in on the large, mostly glass building, surrounded by trees on the edge of campus closest to our apartment—yeah, that wasn't an accident.

Not only had I always loved the campus library—they'd done the remodel on it when I was seventeen, making most of my bookworm fantasies come true—but for the past few months, a rather attractive guy had started to work at the front desk during the morning hours and sometimes late at night. Which—you know—didn't hurt.

Stepping through the glass doors, I was greeted by three lovely things at once: a reprieve from the misty rain, deliciously warm air surrounding me, and the can't-be-beat smell of books.

I stood in the foyer, closed my eyes and breathed it in, but only for a second. I was on a mission.

Walking forward, I sped through the second set of doors into the main building. The library had an extremely tall and angular ceiling, which met up with the great windows. I wasn't normally a huge fan of modern architecture—preferring cozy dark wood and overstuffed chairs to clean lines—but that's where the clean-cut, cold part of the building ended. Everything inside was meant for readers. Couches, chairs, tables, and even a few window seats made for great places to plop down with a good book or take notes for an assignment. There were overhead lights, sure, but each little nook and cranny had a completely unique lamp throwing warm light into the small space.

There were two main floors, but they didn't reach wall to wall, so you could see them both when you entered, like the back of a dollhouse. A beautiful wooden spiral staircase led up to the second floor where they kept the fiction and classic literature. That made for three floors, including the basement where they kept the stacks.

The decor was very Northwest-y, I suppose thanks to good ole Gretta Rosario. She used to be the librarian here before she passed away about six years ago. I only remembered meeting her a few times, but she was a kind, gray-haired, fellow book lover who liked the outdoors as much as she loved reading. She was always looking for ways to bring nature inside. Her husband, the head of a local log-cabin construction company, had made and donated the grand, wooden spiral staircase along with most of the money for the remodel.

He wanted the place to whisper "Gretta." The lamps were actually from their home; Gretta being a funky-lamp collector, setting them up all over their expansive abode.

I'd come to know certain areas of the library by these lamps. Fringy Pink was a great place during the summer because it was light, but not too sunny on hot days due to the large red-budded Rhododendron covering up most of the window next to the floral print lounge chair. Small Dark and Red was in a shadowy corner with a two-seater table, a good date spot—if you were into taking dates to the library, which I was. Over Your Shoulder had to be my favorite year-round reading spot because it was a cushiony window seat set in a bay window on the second floor toward the back of the building. It had a view of the campus gardens, you could hide away there for hours, and it was furnished with a simple floor lamp that peeked over your shoulder, shedding just enough light on the pages. Green Accountant was the best studying place, tucked away between bookshelves in the middle of the first floor, with a large table so you could spread out your textbooks and research.

Today, I wasn't planning on sticking around, having a nine o'clock Dramatic Literature class I needed to get to. I tried to keep my eyes averted from the cute guy sitting at the circulation desk while I skirted past and bounded up the spiral staircase to find a copy of *The Tragedy of Hamlet: Prince of Denmark*.

I found it quickly and flipped it open, searching around a bit until I found the soliloquy. My eyes scanned the text.

"Aha!" I said aloud, and way louder than I should've. My shoulders scrunched up, but a quick glance around assured me no one was nearby.

My finger landed on the page, right next to the word "may." It *was* may, not might! I had been right! And I was rhyming! A smile spread across my face as my fingers clutched the play, about to return it to the shelf. But I stopped.

This was big. If he'd written only that one word wrong, it had to mean something. Maybe he made the mistake on purpose, to send a message. But what seemed even more likely was that this was proof Dr. Campbell hadn't committed suicide, that maybe he was murdered.

A shiver ran down the length of my sweater-covered arms. Chewing on my bottom lip, I realized I needed to let the police know about this. It wasn't that I was trying to be rude in my assumption they had missed the clue, but I seriously doubted anyone other than an English buff would recognize something like this.

I wrinkled my nose at the memory of Detective Valdez's cold demeanor and decided to take the book with me, just in case he needed proof. Though, checking a book out *would* mean I had to go by the front desk.

Tiptoeing to the end of the row of bookshelves, I peered out until I could see *him*. He was sitting on the tall circulation desk stool, swiveling back and forth as he concentrated on the paperback folded in half in his hands. Well, there was one point against the guy. Why did some people always feel the need to strangle books, bending them all the way back?

All I really knew about him was he'd started working here in the summer, which meant I saw him a lot, being a local and—as you may have guessed—a frequenter of the library especially when I had it almost all to myself. I knew his name was Alex. And he'd said hi to me, twice. Also, his hair was thick, wavy, dark, and sometimes when he was reading it would fall onto his forehead like he was Clark Kent's Latin younger brother.

Chewing on my lip as I watched him, I wished I had taken more than six minutes to get myself ready. But just as soon as it came, I shook the thought right out of my head. No. It didn't matter. I wasn't dating any more guys from the university.

It wasn't like I was celibate or anything, I was simply tired of getting serious with guys only to find out their future plans all involved leaving once they graduated. I didn't blame them. I'd simply come to the realization I was different than ninety-nine percent of the student population, having grown up here and planning to stay. For a person who loved Pine Crest and couldn't imagine living anywhere else, the words, "once I move back to..." were a deal breaker. I mean, knowing I was going to lose Liv at the end of this school year was hard enough.

Plus, college was a lot of work. I was super busy with reading and writing essay after essay and... you know... a bunch of other stuff like... taking care of my new dog. My schedule was booked. No time for boyfriends, even ones who have dark brown eyes and skin the color of vintage book pages.

I blinked, bringing myself back to reality. Hamlet. I had the copy and—I checked my watch—only twenty minutes to get to class. Swinging my messenger bag behind me, I headed down the spiral staircase.

Sliding the book forward on the counter, I swallowed as I waited for him to look up.

"Oh, hey," he said, his brown eyes meeting mine.

I smiled and held out my ID card. "Hi."

He put aside his book, laying it flat on its pages, spine straight up as he took my card and scanned the barcode on the back. I cringed, fingers curling into my palms so I might resist reaching out to save the poor, bent book. I did notice he was reading *Slaughterhouse Five* by Kurt Vonnegut and forgave his book-strangling tendencies, slightly.

"Good book," I said, motioning to his crumpled paperback.

"I'm liking it a lot more than I thought I would."

He grabbed the one I was checking out and moved to scan it, but didn't get far. Freezing, he glanced at the title of the play and then looked back at me with narrowed eyes.

"Hamlet?"

I kicked the toes of my sneakers against the circulation desk as I nodded and kept any Shakespeare fangirling at bay. Liv always told me I came on too strong when anyone asked me a question about books. As much as my stomach fluttered excitedly at the prospect of a literary conversation with the cute library guy, I decided to wait and let him ask the questions.

"Is this because of that guest professor who killed himself last night?" he asked.

I sucked in a breath. *Oh, I see. Not a literary conversation after all, just regular campus gossip.* Disappointed in him, but willing to forgive him again, I nodded.

"You hear some amateur found him and messed up the whole crime scene?" He rolled his eyes.

My head shot back, indignant. "Well—um—I hadn't heard *that*. I heard she was shocked and didn't know what she was dealing with at first. Her actions after she figured out he was dead sounded really instinctual, though." I was suddenly very glad I hadn't blurted out it had been me who'd found him and even though I still didn't want him to know, I couldn't help trying to repair my reputation a little if those were the rumors going around.

His shoulders settled as he stared at me. "How do you know it was a 'she' who found the body?"

"I'm an English major. That's my building." I shrugged, hoping he couldn't read my mind.

His gaze deepened for a moment and then his eyes roamed over what he could see of me over the large desk.

"It was you, wasn't it?" he said at last. "You found the body."

5

Shaking my head noncommittally, I said, "I don't know what you're talking about. Can I please have my book now?"

Alex scanned the barcode on the back of the book, keeping an eye on me as he did so. He was moving to hand the book back to me, when his hand stopped. My fingers grabbed at air.

"What?" I asked, letting my hands fall onto the circulation desk in exhaustion.

"How else would you know the connection between what happened last night and Hamlet? Word doesn't travel *that* fast, not even on this campus." He stood up from the stool and pushed his shoulders back as he rose to his full—probably six-feet-something—height.

My fingers tapped on the cool wood of the counter between us as I tried to think. Something he said clicked in my brain.

"If word doesn't travel that fast, how do *you* know about the Hamlet connection?"

His jaw clenched down tight for a moment. My eyes

widened as I recognized that expression. Tall, tan skin, dark eyes, disapproving looks. It all added up. I glanced at the student ID card clipped to the bottom of his blue hooded sweatshirt, visible now he was standing. Alex Valdez.

I gasped and pointed. "You're his son! Detective Valdez is your father. That's how you know, right? You look just like him, you know, especially when you're angry."

"Hold on, hold on. I don't think it's any concern to you who my dad—" His face lit up with realization. "That means I was right. It *was* you."

"Okay, yes. It was me. I found the body."

"And what are you going to do with this copy of the play?" He pulled the book back toward him protectively.

"It's absolutely none of your business."

His forehead wrinkled. "It absolutely is. My father is heading up the investigation."

"And?"

"He doesn't need someone reading the contents of a victim's suicide note to the whole campus."

Frowning, I said, "That's not what I'm going to do with it." I tapped my foot, deciding how much I should tell this Alex character. "I was checking it out so I could show the police, actually."

"What are you going to show them? They already have the note." He shrugged, nodding hello to two students entering the library.

I picked at the hem of my sweater. "Well, I think that's kind of police business, actually. Even though your dad might feel it's okay to discuss a case with you, I don't."

"I am—police, that is. Well, almost." Alex rolled his eyes at me. "I only have a few more credits to take and then I'm going to go to the academy." He stood up even taller as he talked about it.

"Following in Dad's footsteps, huh?" I didn't say it in a teasing sort of way, just thoughtful. It was interesting to meet someone who didn't seem conflicted about following a family profession.

"Yeah. It's pretty much what I've always wanted to do. My mom was a cop, too." His eyes shifted down to the counter and he cleared his throat.

Was. I knew that word all too well, having to use it when I talked about Dad now. It still stung every time. The sullen tone Alex had used made me pretty sure his mom hadn't just found a different profession. He'd lost a parent, like me.

Despite the fact I felt a sad kinship with him, the guy was still looking at me like I was a piece of gum stuck on the bottom of his shoe. I didn't press him with any questions about her.

"So you gonna let me have my book?" I asked, changing the subject.

"I suppose." He sighed. "But really, what do you think this is going to prove?"

Maybe it was his churlish attitude, maybe it reminded me of his father, but something made me feel like I could trust him. I paused for a moment before saying, "Well, the soliloquy was written incorrectly. I mean, it was only one word that was slightly different, but it was bugging me all night and I wanted to come check this morning."

"Didn't trust the internet." He nodded in approval.

"Dr. Campbell was a serious Shakespeare nerd. There's no way he would miss this word. I don't think he committed suicide. I think he might have been..." I leaned in closer and let my eyes widen for effect. "Murdered."

Alex's face didn't tense up like I hoped it would at that word. "Huh. Interesting. Well, I suppose it couldn't hurt to let the police know."

My shoulders dropped in relief. "That's what I was thinking."

Alex handed me the book, finally.

"Thanks," I said and was about to leave when I thought of something else. "Why do you work in the library then? If you're studying to be a cop?"

He shrugged. "I like to read. I was almost done with my courses down in California, so I don't have a full schedule and this gives me a little extra cash," he said. I felt like there was something more, but after a few seconds of silence, it appeared he was going to hold onto it.

Nodding, I pressed my lips together. Alex handed me my ID card back, but not before glancing at it.

"See you around, Pepper."

Smiling back at him, I was thankful he hadn't said anything about my crazy name. I loved being named after my grandma, but I could've done without the teasing growing up and the weird looks now I was older. Also, "Pass the Pepper, please" is only funny like once.

"Thanks, Alex," I said and then left. As I walked, I pulled out my phone and messaged Liv.

"Though he be but hot, he is fierce. #libraryguy"

Liv responded right away.

*"Fierce can be good... *shrugs*"*

I shook my head.

"Not in a smoldery, 'I'm so into you I must eschew the world and it's expectations so I may spend my life fighting for you' way. This was more of an annoyed ferocity."

Liv, used to my longer-than-normal texts, replied quickly.

"Boo. Sorry Peps. :'(Also... you're such a nerd."

I laughed and put my phone away, heading to class.

I DIDN'T GET a break until the afternoon, so by the time I walked into the police station in town, two blocks south of campus and the complete opposite direction from my apartment, I was about to burst with my information.

Ernie Mason was sitting behind the large wooden desk in the foyer. He had been the crossing guard at my elementary school growing up, but after a few close calls—namely with the Joshua brothers and their infamous trucks—he'd decided to move to a safer job while still helping the good people of Pine Crest. He'd been the receptionist at the local police station for the past ten years, at least.

"Why, Pepper Brooks, when did you go and grow up on me?" Ernie walked out from behind the desk and enveloped me in a bear hug, well, maybe a baby bear hug. Ernie was a small man, shorter than my five-foot-five self, and slight as could be. He had a small mustache—which barely covered his thin lip—beady eyes, and a smile as wide as anyone.

"What brings you in here?" His thin eyebrows furrowed together as he let go of me.

"I need to talk with Detective Valdez, Ernie. It's really important."

The entirety of what I knew about criminal investigations was from what I'd read in books, so I didn't know the protocol about interrupting an officer currently working on a case. However, I hoped he would consider a potential murder worthy of an interruption.

Ernie shook his head and tsked. "That new one, huh? Replaced George after he retired, you know. Still can't quite get a read on him." His blue eyes narrowed as he thought about the detective.

"Wait. George retired?" *So that was why he hadn't been there yesterday*. "Gosh, I must be out of the loop. I didn't realize that, or how we'd gotten a new detective in town. When did this happen?"

"Early in the summer." Ernie set a hand softly on my shoulder. "Oh, it's okay, Pepper. You've been dealing with quite a bit in the last year. We understand."

My gaze dropped to my shoes. "Yeah," was all I could get out.

I suppose I *had* been a little out of touch with Pine Crest lately. Heck, I hadn't even known Naked Newt had bought Bittersweet, our local coffee shop and café, from Kathy. Liv and I had been unpleasantly surprised to see him behind the counter the other morning when we'd gone in for our normal fix. Newt was known for starting a new business every few months though, so my guess was he wouldn't last long in the latte and bakery business.

"The detective is in the back, in his office, if you'd like to see him." Ernie motioned behind him with a quick jerk of his head.

I nodded, then I headed down the hall in the direction he'd shown me. Taking a deep breath, I wrapped my fingers around the strap of my messenger bag, buoyed by the knowledge I had the book in my bag for evidence, in case Detective Valdez didn't believe me.

His door was shut, so I knocked.

"Come in." The words were barked out from behind the glass and I opened it, slipping inside before I changed my mind.

Growing up in a close-knit community, where everyone had known me since I was in diapers and remembered when I used to make daisy necklaces for people, definitely spoiled a person. I wasn't used to adults who didn't smile when they saw me or comment nostalgically about a time when I'd done something particularly adorable years earlier.

Detective Valdez looked at me like I was a nuisance instead of a town treasure. And it flustered me a bit.

"Hey, um—how are you, Detective Valdez?" I stammered, closing the door behind me.

It took a good few seconds before he glanced up from his computer screen again. A good few seconds I spent growing more and more nervous, more and more unsure of myself. What the heck had I been thinking? Of course the police wouldn't want some random college student's help on a suicide/murder case. I shook my head and was about to pretend like I had somewhere else to be right then when he turned his attention to me.

"Hello." His dark eyes narrowed for a moment. "Ms. Brooks was it?"

I nodded.

"And how can I help you? You forget something?"

Tipping my head to the side, I said, "Well, not exactly forget, more like didn't realize until this morning." I pulled the book from my messenger bag and flipped to the soliloquy. "You see, detective, I've been memorizing Hamlet's soliloquy for fun. Fergie said something the other week about how not enough people memorize things these days and our brains are all going to mush because our phones do everything for us. Well, that's why I moved his hand."

I suddenly remembered Alex saying I had ruined the whole crime scene. Those had probably been his father's words first. I didn't look up, knowing the detective's dark stare would only make me more nervous.

Swallowing, I continued. "I think it's why the line caught my eye in the first place, I'd been so focused on those words the last week."

Detective Valdez lifted his hands from the desk and opened them. "And?"

Yep, he was still wholly uninterested in me and unamused by how I'd interrupted whatever it was he'd been so focused on before I'd come in.

"It was wrong," I blurted the statement before I could chicken out.

The detective's eyebrows lifted, but he didn't show any other interest besides that. "What was wrong, Miss Brooks?" He looked like he was already thinking he didn't have time for me, for this, for whatever was going to come out of my mouth next.

My fingers curled into fists in my lap. "He didn't kill himself. He was murdered—I think. He wrote down the Hamlet soliloquy incorrectly. It said 'might' not 'may.' He just—well, a professor who specialized in Shakespearean analysis wouldn't do that, especially not if they were planning on killing themselves. Those things take time and consideration… I'm told."

Valdez ran his hand across his smoothly shaven chin. He was the kind of guy who didn't seem like he would ever let himself get a two o'clock shadow, let alone five.

"We already know he didn't commit suicide, Miss Brooks," he said at last.

My breath caught in my throat.

6

"Wait. You do?" I leaned forward. The man was actually taking me seriously.

But as soon as my excitement came, it disappeared. *He already knew about the clue?* Did that mean...? *Alex.* Had he come here and told his dad what I'd divulged to him earlier this morning? Would anyone stoop so low?

Anger burned in my chest. *Curse being a rule follower and not wanting to skip classes. That sneak had beat me here.*

Unaware I was thinking terrible thoughts about his son, Valdez watched me.

"Er—oh. Well—so you know about it already. Good." I nodded.

The detective's jaw clenched tight as he returned the gesture, making me think, once again, of Alex. The guy was even more of a jerk than I'd first thought. He'd acted as if I had been inconveniencing *him*, all the while he was stealing *my* evidence so he could come in here and look like the hero of the day.

I stood up abruptly, fingers curling around the strap of my messenger bag.

"Sorry to waste your time, then." I grimaced and got myself out of there.

I felt about three feet tall after my encounter with the detective. And maybe if I had been feeling like a bigger person, I wouldn't have immediately started making a plan to confront his lying, evidence-poaching son. But as it was, I let the anger stew and my humiliation grow throughout the night and my classes the next day.

Evilsworth was my last class of the day, so I was feeling pretty ready to punch something by the time I made my way to the library that evening. Plus, I wasn't only there for confrontation, but had a large paper due next week and was hoping to get the majority of it written while I waited.

I pushed my way through the glass doors of the library, my research papers and books stuffed in my bag alongside a peanut butter and banana sandwich, and a thermos of half coffee, half hot chocolate. If Green Accountant was open, that was where I was headed. Not only was it surrounded by enough bookshelves to hide my illegal homemade mocha and scarf down my food, but it would give me a good vantage point for peeking out periodically to see if Alex had started his shift.

Rounding the bookshelf where the large table held the green accountant's lamp, I stopped as I noticed papers and books already strewn across the wooden surface. Two students from Evilsworth's class sat there, most likely working on the same paper I was there to write.

"Oh hey, Pepper." Trish waved at me, looking up from her laptop.

"Long time, no see," Heather joked.

I smiled and stepped closer to them, though I didn't sit. I didn't want to be rude, but I worked best when I was alone.

"Hey!" I made my voice bright and personable.

"Boy, was Evensworth on a roll of terror today." Heather rolled her eyes.

I kicked at the old carpet with the toe of my shoe. "Right? I mean, could he have been more disrespectful about Dr. Campbell? He didn't even seem sad when he mentioned it in class yesterday."

Heather's eyebrows rose and she leaned forward. "Yeah, probably because he was the one who killed the guy. Katie told me he and the dead guy had some huge fight right before he died."

My throat felt suddenly dry with this news.

"Besides the fact he's a total jerk, why would Evensworth fight with some random professor from Oxford?" Trish asked the question I was thinking, but hadn't been able to ask. In my surprise, I barely felt like I could breathe, let alone talk.

"You know that new book Evensworth just wrote, the one he can't go two minutes without talking about?"

Trish scoffed. "Oh, yeah. Something about 'American Literature: A New Frontier.' Boring."

I nodded, mirroring her sentiment.

"Well, apparently, an article came out two days ago where Dr. Campbell completely ripped the book apart. I think he even used the phrase, 'unsubstantiated drivel' at one point."

My heart hammered in my chest. *First I figure out Dr. Campbell was murdered and now I have evidence that points toward a very likely suspect.* As concentrated on the soliloquy clue as I'd been, I hadn't even thought about *who* might've murdered the professor. My toes scrunched uncomfortably in my sneakers as I thought of a killer on the loose around campus.

"Hey, I've gotta get going on this paper, so…" I waved

quickly as I backed away before they could invite me to work with them.

A shiver ran down my spine at the memory of seeing Naked Newt on campus right before I'd found the body. He'd said that creepy thing about blood being on the wind. Newt said gross stuff all the time, though. That didn't make him a killer. Probably. Plus, it sounded like Evilsworth was building quite the case against himself. I searched for another place to sit as I contemplated what I'd heard.

Unfortunately, Small Dark and Red was occupied, along with all of my favorite spots, left me plopping my butt down on the leather couch near the front entrance.

Great.

Now, not only would it look like I was literally stalking Alex, waiting for him to come in to work—which, I know I *technically* was—but being out in the open also meant I was going to have to be really stealthy if I wanted to eat my dinner and drink from my thermos.

Ginger, an education major, was working the counter at the moment and she smiled up at me as I arranged my books and papers around me. She was nice, if not a little confusing, being one of those people who smiled too much and always seemed happy no matter what. She also had blond hair which, matched with her name, made her seem like an oxymoron to me.

I pulled out my laptop, turned off the WiFi so I wouldn't be tempted to "internet," and I got to work. Ginger didn't seem to notice as I snuck bites of my sandwich from my bag. Or maybe she did, but felt bad about how my papers blew all over the place each time someone opened the front door so she was letting me get away with it.

Once I got into the flow of my writing, however, I stopped noticing when things shifted slightly in the wind.

Seeing each paragraph connect back to my thesis always felt like some kind of magic and I was amazed each time I was able to make it happen.

Which was why I didn't notice the dark shadow looming over me until the owner of said shadow cleared his throat.

Jumping, I glanced up. I had also, apparently, stopped caring about hiding my sandwich, because the last quarter hung from my mouth as I gazed up. My fingers grabbed at it and stuffed the rest inside my maw. Blinking, I met Alex's stony glare.

"Pepper." His thick eyebrows rose as he looked down on me, both literally and metaphorically.

I had about three bites too many in my mouth and all I could do was chew the sticky concoction awkwardly as Alex watched.

After an agonizing amount of time—I don't even want to guess how long it lasted—I swallowed and said, "Alex."

"What'd they say about the clue?"

If I hadn't just crammed a bunch of bread in my mouth, I would've scoffed. As it was, I didn't want to add "spat a bunch of crumbs" to the list of weird things I'd done in front of Alex. So I settled for craning my neck forward and giving him my best "are you serious?" scowl.

"You should know," I said after one last swallow to make sure all of the sandwich pieces were out of my mouth.

Confusion drew lines across his face as he said, "I told you I'm not a full cop yet. I'm not actually on the case."

"Yeah, right. Except you apparently called him to tell him my clue before I could."

Alex sighed. "I have no idea what you're talking about and I don't have time for this. I've gotta go relieve Ginger so she can get something to eat."

He walked back to the circulation desk, then waved

goodbye to Ginger as she grabbed her things.

Okay, now I was confused. Alex hadn't told his dad my clue?

I pulled my thermos out from my bag and chugged some of the warm drink before I moved enough papers and books around so I could stand up. Then I walked over to the desk, eyes looking just about everywhere but at Alex's serious face.

My fingertip squished down on a circle of paper which must've escaped from a three-hole punch somewhere.

"So... you *didn't* tell your dad my clue?" I squinted one eye and tried to look at Alex indirectly, as if he were the sun during an eclipse.

He shook his head. "Why would I do that?"

"When I went to tell him, he already knew about it."

Alex shrugged. "He is the lead detective. Ever consider that maybe he's doing his job?"

I let my gaze drop to the counter again. "Sorry. I thought... It didn't seem like something police officers would've caught. When he told me they already knew Dr. C had been murdered, I thought you'd said something."

"Well, I didn't." Alex paused, making me look up into his brown eyes. "To be honest, they probably didn't know about the Shakespeare stuff. I bet they got the toxicology report back or something else clued them into the fact he wasn't killed by the pills."

My eyes widened. "Wait. He wasn't killed by the pills? How do you know?"

Alex's head fell to the side as if he was tired of dealing with me. "If they think it was murder then the pills can't be the cause of death. I mean, murderers usually don't force pills down people's throats. And it sounds like there weren't any signs of a struggle." A smirk pulled at the corner of his mouth. "Unless you changed the crime scene so much they couldn't tell."

"Haha." My brain was going over this whole "murder" thing too much to give in to Alex's ribbing. I leaned in close, chewing on my lip for a moment before saying, "Some of my classmates heard about a professor getting in a fight with the guy before he died." I gestured over my shoulder toward Green Accountant and narrowed my eyes.

Alex leaned in close, mirroring my facial expression. "You don't say?"

His breath smelled like peppermint and I got a waft of clean laundry in lieu of cologne. It made me want to close my eyes until I remembered how he was surly and frustrating and how I wasn't dating guys from school.

"A few students think they know who the murderer is without knowing any of the clues or being involved with the investigation at all?" As his tone flattened and I realized he was mocking me, I pulled myself back, mad he'd fooled me into thinking he cared about my information. "Hurry, let's go find them and arrest their suspect right away."

By the time he'd finished, Alex's voice was so deadpan I would've thought all humor had left his body if it hadn't been for the mischievous spark in his eyes.

I put my hands up. "Okay, okay. I get it. You don't think it's important. You don't have to be rude." I shot him a sharp look and turned to leave.

"You know there's no eating in the library, Pepper." His words stopped me.

I smirked at the playfulness in his tone and then kept walking, making sure to take an extra long drink from my thermos when I sat again.

After another half hour of work on my essay, I packed up my things and headed out, waving a quick goodbye to

Alex as I passed him. He grunted something and dipped his chin in response.

The apartment was dark when I got home, save for a small yellow lamp in the kitchen. As I stripped off my coat and set my bag down on the couch, Hamburger barked and waggled excitedly around my feet. My phone buzzed in my pocket while I was scratching Hammy's ears. It was a text from Liv.

"Wanna meet me and the Js for drinks?"

Liv's business friends all had names that started with J. There was Jenna, James, and Justin. She called them the Js for short, since they were usually together. And I liked them, but it didn't seem right to be out having fun so soon after what had happened.

Thinking of the deceased Dr. Campbell, my mind returned to Fergie and wondered how she was holding up. Checking my watch, I grabbed Hammy's leash. Fergie was usually in her office at night, and even if she wasn't, Ham and I could at least get in a good walk. I replied to Liv's text.

"Thanks, but I'm out tonight. Say hey to the Js for me."

She answered right back.

"I'll only allow it if you spill about mean/cute library guy. Jenna says she saw you talking to him again. I told her you weren't interested, but she seemed to think your body language said otherwise."

I bit my lip. Jenna rarely came to the library, which meant she probably saw me talking to Alex through the window. And if she'd misread what I was feeling toward him…

"Deal, but seriously don't get your hopes up."

I grabbed my jacket and pulled it back on, hooking Hammy's leash onto her collar.

Literally Dead

Hamburger's nails click-click-clicked on the concrete as we walked down the campus pathways. I wrapped her leash around my arm and then shoved both hands deep into the downy pockets of my jacket. She stopped to smell something every seven-and-a-half steps and barked at anything that moved—plus a few things that didn't—and yanked me around like she was trying to give me longer arms. But every few moments, she would look up at me adoringly, tongue lolling out the side of her mouth and I couldn't help but giggle.

I figured it was late enough no one would really care if Hammy came into the building. Plus, Fergie had been asking to meet her, so this would be a great time. The campus was empty save for a few people out walking the cool, lamp-lit pathways, and by the time I reached the edge of campus, Ham and I were alone.

As I passed through the doors of the English building, I reached down and scooped up the little dog, tucking her under my arm as we continued inside. Hamburger pressed her body up against mine and looked around wildly, until we reached the hallway where Dad's—er—Fergie's office was housed. Right as I rounded the corner, Hammy's ears perked up and a low growl rumbled through her body.

"Whoa, girl. What's wrong?" I asked.

I got my answer in the form of a person appearing rather than an answer from my dog. Detective Valdez stopped in the doorway. His eyes, already dark and focused, surveyed me and then the growling Hamburger.

"Miss Brooks," he said, tipping his head forward, and then he turned to leave.

My mouth hung open, unsure what to say. Why was he here? I peeked through the door, into Fergie's open office and saw her sitting there, head in her hands. Oh no. Had he just broken the news to her about Dr. C's murder-not-suicide?

I rushed forward, so glad I'd come. This was no time for the woman to be alone.

"Fergie?" I said as I knocked softly on the door.

Tears sliding down her face, she glanced up. "Oh! Pepper, what are you doing here?"

"I thought I'd come check on you and let you meet my new dog, the one I was telling you about."

Fergie swiped at her teary face and stood. "Goodness! She has the face of a radio star, doesn't she?" The older woman patted Hammy's stubby, wrinkly snout.

I laughed.

"And what is her name?" Fergie asked.

"Hamburger," I said quietly, then cleared my throat. "My niece named her." I shrugged.

Fergie took Ham's paw in her hand and shook it. "Hamburguesa, lovely to meet you." When I gave her a funny look, she said, "It's Spanish, dear. A more lady-like option, if you're ever in want of one."

I smiled. Hamburguesa. I mentally added it to the dog's list of nicknames.

"Everything okay?" I asked, tentatively.

Fergie's eyes teared up again. "Oh, Pepper. No. Everything is *not* okay."

"So you know it was murder?" My forehead creased together as I watched her body sag from sadness.

She nodded slowly. "I know. But that's not even the worst of it." Her blue eyes met mine, an intensity gripping them I'd not seen before. Her hand clasped down over mine as she said, "Pepper, Detective Valdez was just here questioning me. I'm quite sure I'm their prime suspect."

7

My eyes widened as I took in the information. Hammy squirmed in my arms, so I set her down on the floor, holding tight to her leash as she sniffed around the room.

"You? A suspect? But—but don't they know you? You wouldn't hurt anyone, let alone your good friend."

Fergie's bony fingers squeezed down on mine. "I'm glad to hear you think so highly of me, dear, but unfortunately, it seems the evidence is stacking against me."

I pulled in a deep breath. "What evidence?"

"Well, they wouldn't tell me, so this is purely speculation, but he was found in my office, there's no one to substantiate my alibi since I was alone, I'm the only one here who knew him well at all, and…" her voice petered out and she cleared her throat. "Then there's our history together."

"History? Together?" I asked.

Fergie let go of my hand and paced away, her flowy clothing wafting behind her as if she were the ghost of the murdered king in a stage production of *The Tragedy of*

Hamlet: Prince of Denmark. "We were somewhat of an item, for a while—off and on."

I thought for a moment about how flustered Fergie had looked when I'd run into Stephanie and her in the hallway before going in to check on Dr. Campbell. Was Fergie often dramatic? Sure. Disorganized? Absolutely. But the woman was always self-assured. The doubt I'd seen in her eyes during those moments in the hall was something I'd not experienced when looking at her before.

There was a tiny, minuscule, fraction of a second where I actually entertained the idea that maybe my favorite teacher had done it, had offed an old lover and colleague. Then she turned and her worried eyes met mine, and that thought disappeared for good. No. The kindness she'd shown me—heck, everyone she met—pointed to a woman who would never hurt anyone.

My shoulders relaxed slightly. "Don't worry, Dr. Ferguson. They'll see it wasn't you. They just have to look at *all* of the evidence."

The old woman slumped into the chair in the corner, the gauzy fabrics making her look like a liquid the way she spilled into the thing. "I hope you're right." Her voice sounded worn without the vibrant, operatic timber I was used to.

Hammy tugged on the leash, pulling my attention from my professor for a moment. The dog had been snorting around, sniffing the floor, skittering this way and that around the desk, but now she had her whole face buried in Fergie's purse.

"Oh, no. Hammy, no." I lunged forward.

Pulling her head free of the bag, I noticed she'd gotten a hold of something. My fingers pried open her little jaw, and I saw a piece of crumpled paper, slightly wet from doggie saliva. I pulled the thing out of her mouth and unfolded it. It was only about the size of my hand, fully opened. The ink was smudged from being wet, but other than that, the wording was clear.

And it sent a shiver down my spine.

It was the same handwriting I'd seen on the note under Dr. C's hand. And it had been in Fergie's purse? Unlike the soliloquy, which became messier, more rushed, as it went on, these few lines were neat as could be, measured.

Be this the whetstone of your sword. Let grief convert to anger. Blunt not the heart, enrage it.

Face crinkled in worry, I stood.

"What's that?" Fergie asked from her chair.

"Hammy was eating this, but..." I shook my head. "It's..." I held it up. "It's Shakespeare, I think. You didn't write this?"

While it was in her purse, it wasn't Dr. Ferguson's handwriting, which was like none I'd ever seen: long, stretched out, delicate cursive that mirrored the soft, wispiness of the long scarves she always draped over her body.

This writing was tall, straight, still cursive, but there was a tightness to it the likes of which I don't think had ever existed in my favorite professor. But the note *had* been in the woman's purse...

Fergie stood and walked over, reading over my shoulder as I flattened the wet and crumpled piece of paper.

"Macbeth," she said and then shook her head. "No, dear. I did not write that."

Was she lying to me? She didn't seem to be phased by the note, didn't seem to recognize it...

I repeated the title in my head. *Macbeth.* I knew from reading the play it was a bloody story full of backstabbing and revenge. I wouldn't expect any excerpts from it to be light or happy, but still, the words on the paper made my heart hammer out of fear.

"Fergie, if you didn't write this, why is it in your purse?"

The woman arched her eyebrows. "It could've been left over from when we did the Scottish play. Who knows with that land-yacht of a purse. I'm always surprised at what I find in there."

I swallowed. Technically, Fergie was right. Random pieces of paper carrying Shakespeare quotes floating around in her purse was not out of the realm of possibility. Which would explain why she wasn't freaking out like I was. She hadn't seen the note left under Dr. Campbell's body. She didn't know the handwriting was the same. I kept that fact to myself, however, not wishing to alarm the already disturbed woman.

"Is it just me or does this sound kind of threatening?" I asked, trying a less direct approach.

"Malcom, I believe," she muttered to herself. "Yes, yes, it's a very threatening line, dear. It's during the scene when MacDuff learns his wife and children have been slaughtered. Malcom is telling him to use his hatred, fuel it and turn it into revenge."

As she spoke, Fergie's shoulders squared and she stood taller. It sounded as if she were a director, giving direction to one of her actors.

Even though Fergie seemed a little better, bolstered by the escape into the words of her beloved Bard, I couldn't help but feel worse at her analysis. I was sure now she hadn't written it—why would she implicate herself by telling me it was a line between two bloody scenes?—and my mind latched onto the only other option: someone had put it in Fergie's purse. The word "revenge" stuck in my throat like my sandwich had when I'd shoved too much of it in at once earlier in the library. What if the killer had been trying to hurt Fergie and got Dr. C instead?

"There isn't anyone who might've been upset with you or Dr. Campbell? Is there?" I remembered back to the conversation I'd had in the library about Evilsworth. He would've been equally mad at Fergie as he was at Dr. Campbell since she was the one who brought him here in the first place.

"Oh, I don't think so. He was a brilliant man. Sometimes he could be a little short with people, blunt to a fault, some may say." She waved her hand at me. "But he had the sweetest heart, my Davis."

I noticed she hadn't answered the part about anyone being mad at her, but she appeared tired and my heart ached for her, so I let it go for now. Stuffing the paper in my pocket, I scooped up Hammy and reached out for Fergie's bony hand.

"I'm so sorry for your loss, Fergie. I really am." I squeezed tight. "I'm sure the police will figure out the truth and will bring the killer to justice."

Fergie smiled sadly. "Thank you, Pepper. And thank you for your visit. I think I will finish up here and head home." She moved toward her desk, but then paused, walked gingerly around the chair, and then stacked a few papers together. "And I think I'll need to talk to them about getting me a different chair." She placed a long finger to her lips. "Or maybe the whole desk should go."

Sighing, I waved and headed out of her office. I couldn't imagine having to continue working in an office where someone you had once loved—or maybe still did—had been killed. I found it hard enough to walk by Dad's old office, and he had died of natural causes.

My free hand, the one that wasn't holding onto

Hamburger, searched in my pocket for the paper. Sure of its existence, but unsure of what to do with it, I set Hammy down on the ground and put us on a course for home. Darkness curled around us and I decided on a longer, more well-lit path, over my normal route. It'd been a long day, but there was a potential murderer wandering around on campus and I wasn't about to take any chances. Plus, my head felt full and jumbled; maybe a longer walk would help clear things up.

On one hand, I felt so sure Fergie wasn't the suspect the police should be looking into. But on the other, this note had been in her purse. And then there was her odd behavior the day Dr. C had been killed.

A cool breeze whipped past me as I passed the bright student center where the cafeteria and gym were located. The sharp scent of burning leaves rode on the wind, remnants from someone cleaning up their yard, no doubt. I sighed and took a turn down a winding path that wove through a grouping of freshmen dorms. The smell of more burning foliage—a different kind of leaf—always sat heavy in this part of campus. Hammy snorted, nose high in the air as she caught a whiff of the skunky scent. I shook my head and let my thoughts return to the note.

One thing was sure. If I turned this in, and they were already suspecting Fergie, it would be some terrible nail in the coffin of the case against her.

And even though I trusted the police to do their jobs, these weren't just the same old blood and fingerprints kind of clues they were used to dealing with. This killer was leaving behind clues, knowingly or not, using literature.

I pulled my coat tighter around me as a chill danced down my spine at the thought of the murderer. My eyes darted around me in between the dark buildings. The creepy feeling reminded me again of my run-in with Naked Newt just before I'd found Dr. C. It was way more likely he'd killed the man than Fergie. And then there was Evilsworth and what Trish and Heather had told me about his beef with the visiting professor.

Turning right on my street, I sucked in a deep breath and made a decision. Maybe the police didn't need my help, but I was pretty sure my favorite professor did.

THE NOTE SAT in my pocket like a lead weight the next morning as I headed onto campus to research winter quarter classes at the registrar's office. The paper was made even heavier by the knowledge that, by keeping this away from the police, I was officially breaking the law, obstructing justice.

I sighed, shaking my head slowly, looking from the rock to the hard place I was stuck in between.

Inside the office, I grabbed a course catalog from the files hanging on the wall and began to flip through to the English section. My eyes caught on the pictures of the faculty hanging on the wall in front of me. I couldn't help but smile at Fergie's photograph. She even managed to look dramatic in the picture, one eyebrow higher than the other, a mischievous grin plastered on her face. Not a cell in her body was that of a murderer. Then my gaze found Evilsworth's picture. His eyes looked like they were disappointed with me even through the camera lens. He had a crooked nose and a hard, thin mouth. I definitely couldn't say the same of him as I had of Fergie.

"Dollar for your thoughts?" someone asked over my right shoulder, entirely too close to my ear.

I jumped, heart beating wildly in my chest as my head whipped around.

Alex stood behind me, hands shoved in his jeans pockets, a light gray hoodie sitting easily on his tall frame. There was a slight twinkle in his eye and he twitched up one eyebrow much like Fergie's in her picture.

I took the course catalog in my hands and swatted it at him. "You scared me half to death, man!"

He chuckled, but so lightly it was more of an exhale. His hands raised in an I'm-innocent way. "Sorry, didn't know you were so jumpy."

Narrowing my eyes, I said, "There's a killer on the loose, you know. This is not the time to be sneaking up on people."

"I didn't sneak. I can't help it if you were staring longingly at a professor you have some crush on and didn't hear me."

My face twisted in disgust. "Eww. A crush? Never." A shiver ran up and down my body. "Wait, isn't it only a penny?"

"What?"

"You said, 'Dollar for your thoughts?' Isn't it supposed to be a penny?"

Alex's face lit up. "Oh, yeah. Whatever was going through your head seemed to be worth more than a penny, though." He shrugged.

I rolled my eyes at him to hide the delighted smiled pulling at the corner of my lips. "Haha." I took a step back, suddenly aware I could smell his fresh-laundry and mint smell.

He tipped his head toward me. "But seriously. Care to share what you were thinking about?"

I sighed, hating the turmoil of doubts and fears roiling about in my poor head. I'd always been a rule follower. I mean, in a small town, your parents are going to hear about anything you do, so… and keeping this piece of evidence secret was feeling like an increasingly worse idea. At that thought, my eyes widened. Alex was pretty much the police. Maybe he could help me decide what to do.

I thought about it, then nodded. "Well, I—it's just that I —" Ugh, I couldn't seem to get it out without it sounding like I was a total criminal. "This." I finally pulled the paper out of my pocket and shoved it toward him.

Alex looked closely at the wrinkly piece of paper. "What am I looking at here?"

"It's the same handwriting as the note I saw with the…" I stopped myself, about to say, "body." I cleared my throat. "With Dr. Campbell."

"Where'd you get it?" His voice tightened along with his grip on the paper.

My fingers itched to grab it back. Okay, showing Alex may *not* have been the best idea.

When I didn't answer his question, Alex shot me an impatient look.

"I—uh—found it," I stammered.

Alex leaned back, standing up straight, and crossed his arms in front of his chest. He didn't have to say anything more, his narrowed eyes spoke quite clearly of his insistence for a better answer.

"Fine, I found it in Fergie's office…" I let the sentence hang there, not wanting to finish it.

"So it's evidence then." Alex raised his eyebrows.

"Yeah." I sighed.

"Which means you should give it to the police. Your professor friend might be in danger if the murderer is still on the loose, leaving notes like this. Is it possible the person could've been trying to get to her and got Dr. Campbell by accident?"

"I don't know," I said. "The hard part is I didn't know Dr. Campbell, so I don't know if he had any enemies, anyone who would've wanted to do him harm. And I can't think of anyone who would dislike Fergie, let alone hurt her."

"Still, you'd better be safe and hand this over to my dad." He pushed the piece of paper back into my hand.

I stared at it for a moment.

Alex's shoulders dropped as he watched my hesitation. "But you're worried it could be used against her, since I'm guessing she's also a suspect?"

I nodded.

Alex reached forward and for a moment I thought he was trying to snatch the note from me, but then his large hand settled over mine.

"Pepper, is this her handwriting?" His voice was kinder, softer than I'd ever heard it. The normal tightness in his dark eyes loosened.

I shook my head.

"Do you think there's any way she could've killed that man?" he asked.

More shaking.

"Then this could mean your teacher is in danger and you have to show someone."

This time I nodded. He was right.

"Where in the professor's office did you find this?" Alex asked.

"Her purse." My words were a tiny mouse, peeking out of hiding, away from safety.

"What?"

A guy down the hallway glanced over at us, alarmed by the sudden burst of volume as the word shot out of Alex.

He leaned closer to me. "What?" It was more like a whisper this time—if a whisper and a yell had some strange lovechild.

"It may have been in her purse, but she didn't recognize it. Even told me it was from a really bad part in Macbeth, a part all about revenge. Why would she tell me that if she was trying to hide it?" Now it was my turn to forcibly whisper.

"I don't know. That's why they're *murderers*; their heads aren't right. Normal people, people who are easy to understand, don't kill people as a way to solve a problem."

"Fine." I turned on my heel. "I'll turn it in."

"And stop getting involved in this case, Pepper. I'm serious. It could be really dangerous."

I waved the course catalog over my shoulder at him as I left, adding next quarter's classes to the list of things I was still unsure about.

8

I'm not proud to admit how much I wanted to do the exact opposite of what Alex had suggested, but in the end, rationality won out and I decided he was right.

I visited Detective Valdez in between classes that day, gave him the second note I'd found, and mentally shut the door on this whole ordeal.

The truth was, I wasn't Nancy Drew's fake sister. I may have figured out some small clue within a Shakespeare quote, but the police hadn't needed it after all—Detective Valdez would neither admit nor deny if it had been the toxicology report that had convinced them, but I saw him shift in his chair uncomfortably when I brought it up, so I was pretty sure that's what it was. These people were professionals. They knew what they were doing and they didn't need some literature loving twenty-one-year-old running around thinking she was part of their group.

Everyone's good at something. The police were obviously good at this investigating stuff. I was good at reciting random lines from classics and having literary analysis debates. And it was probably best if we stuck to what we knew best.

This revelation also helped me make a final decision about my major. I really loved literature. It was my *thing*. And sure I would have to work my butt off for the rest of my career to prove to myself I deserved all of the wonderful opportunities I'd been given because of my family. But becoming a professor at NWU wouldn't be a cakewalk, even with my dad's influence. After graduating with my Bachelor's it would mean enrolling right away in a Master's program and someday a Doctorate. It would mean writing books about my subject. It would mean a lot of late nights after long days. And I was ready to put in the work.

Liv had been right. English was in my blood.

I felt liberated once I came to the decision. I hadn't realized how much it had been weighing on my mind lately, but it felt like I'd taken the equivalent of Fergie's huge copy of *The Complete Works of William Shakespeare* off my shoulders. When I'd told Liv the good news, she danced around the apartment and exclaimed she was making me lasagna to celebrate.

I laughed and let her have her moment. Actually, I was pretty excited, too. When I was done getting all of the degrees I would need, Fergie and I could be colleagues. Working with her would be a dream, one that could've only been topped by getting the chance to work alongside my father.

So I had a smile on my face while I was walking Hammy that evening, before my Liv-made dinner, after all of my classes were done. The campus was bustling with students needing to get here or there and some who were chatting and soaking up the rare fall sunshine. There was a light, green smell in the air which almost seemed like a tease, knowing we wouldn't get that new, just shooting out of the soft earth, growing-plant scent much in the winter months to come when the northwest zipped itself up into a down coat of fog, drizzle, and gray.

So it was with a skip in my step that I passed a guy handing out copies of The *Frond*, a tongue-in-cheek—and often controversial—campus chronicle named after the ferns that grew abundantly in this climate. I normally didn't read the thing, not needing the satirical gossip articles to tell me the buzz on campus. I was a Pine Crest resident, after all, which meant I usually knew about things before people on campus did—the townspeople were always the first to know the best information. But the headline today—which usually didn't stop me in my tracks—made me feel like I had swallowed a bug.

Or maybe it was the grainy picture of a frazzled Fergie on the front page.

Either way, my abrupt stop caught Hammy by surprise and she jerked to a halt. My fingers snatched at the paper so forcefully the guy who had been holding it let out a shocked, "Hey!" I waved my hand dismissively at him while scanning the front page story.

The headline, "Foul-Play Ferguson" atop the article brazenly implicated Dr. Ferguson as the most likely suspect in Dr. Campbell's death. My blood started to boil as I read further.

I hadn't brought my wallet with me, however, so after a moment more I had to hand the paper back to the sour-looking paper guy. My brain was a frenzy as I clicked my tongue at Hammy and she trotted after me, back to the apartment.

When I whirled inside a few minutes later, Liv had music blaring from her phone on the counter. She swayed her hips from side to side as she stirred the ingredients in the skillet. Not even the delicious smell of browning meat, garlic, and sautéed onions could release my lips from the thin line they'd pressed into since seeing that headline. Hearing me enter, Liv turned around.

"Hey, why the weird face? I thought we were celebrating." She pointed her spatula at me. An onion fell from it to the kitchen floor and she bent over to toss it in the garbage.

I unhooked Hammy from her leash and slumped into one of the stools at our breakfast bar. "Just second-guessing my decision."

Now it was Liv's turn to look downtrodden. "But you just..." Her words petered out as if she was too tired to continue. She stirred the meat in the frying pan dejectedly.

Rolling my eyes at her, I said, "Pull it together, lady. I didn't mean my decision about my major. I'm talking about the investigation."

Liv straightened up. "Oh my gosh. I'm so glad. I don't think I could handle listening to anymore of your complaining about this."

I picked up a pen sitting next to me on the counter and threw it at her. "Like I haven't sat through countless hours listening to you lament about everyone's lack of conference-call etiquette."

She stuck her tongue out at me and I washed my hands so I could help.

"So what about the investigation?" she asked, blowing on a spoonful of sauce and then tasting it.

"Well, I *had* decided to stay out of it." I sighed, pulling a large glass baking dish out of the cupboard for the lasagna. "But Fergie is the main suspect and I hate to think of her imprisoned in the viewless winds and blown with restless violence round about the pendant world."

My roommate arched an eyebrow. "Yeah, if they find her guilty, those winds aren't going to be the only place she'll be imprisoned."

I rolled my eyes at her.

"But seriously," she said after a moment. "Romeo aside, you've got a point."

"Claudio." I cleared my throat.

"Whatever. If the police already have her in mind, maybe they're missing other suspects."

I washed the dishes as Liv layered the noodles, ricotta, sauce, and meat into the dish. We talked about our classes while Hammy sniffed around at our feet hoping for rogue ingredients. Doubts swam around in my brain and I realized I'd gotten out of one "To be or not to be" dilemma only to get stuck in a new one.

"To be involved in the investigation or not to be involved in the investigation. That is the *new* question," I said, mumbling the last part.

Liv elbowed me. "Oh please, this one's even less of a question than the last. Of course you're gonna be involved."

Squinting at her, I said, "How are you so sure?"

"You always say how you wish you could do something on your own, apart from your family. Here's your chance. Not to mention you could save a life or at least your favorite professor's reputation, if you succeed." She shrugged as she slid the lasagna into the oven.

Motioning over to the table, she grabbed one of the pads of paper we used to write down grocery lists.

"Let's write down what you know." Liv popped off the lid to a pen and scrawled *The Case of the Shakespeare Nerd* across the top line.

I smirked. "Okay. Well, I found him at six thirty. Fergie

and Stephanie had passed me in the hallway a few minutes before."

Nodding, Liv wrote "Suspects" under the time six thirty and listed Dr. Ferguson and Stephanie underneath in her computer-like perfect printing.

"Whoa, whoa. Wait. Those two aren't suspects. That's why I'm doing this in the first place, to stop the police from arresting Fergie."

Liv tipped her head to the side. "Peps, if you're going to be serious about this, you have to be able to rule Fergie out using facts instead of feelings. We're only putting her on the list to be thorough."

I nodded. Nancy Drew would've done the same. "Okay. Put Naked Newt and Evilsworth next."

Liv eyed me. "Naked Newt? What does he have to do with it?"

"I saw him right before on campus, by the English building. Plus he said something about the scent of blood being on the wind." I cringed, replaying his words in my head.

"When does anything Newt does make sense? Plus, he talks about blood all the time. Come to think of it, he mentioned it this morning when I was getting a mocha before class." Liv waved a hand toward me, trying to dismiss my fears.

I scrunched my nose. "I guess…"

"Well, it can't hurt to write him on the list." She shrugged and added the other two names. "Now we have to look at motives."

"Well, Evilsworth had the best one. Apparently Dr. C had ripped his new book apart in an article. That's enough reason to be mad at someone, to try to get revenge." I recounted what I'd heard from my classmates in the library.

"Yeah," Liv tipped her head to the side. "Killing

someone over a book seems a little intense, even for Evilsworth, but I'll write it down."

Scrunching up my nose, I scoffed. "Maybe that wasn't the only article, though. Maybe it was only the first of many reviews Dr. Campbell planned on writing. This was Evilsworth's chance to stop him from doing so."

"I'm not adding that until we know for sure." Liv shook her head.

Inwardly grumbling, I conceded. "Okay. Fergie and Dr. C used to date, but I'm not so sure that's a motive. She still seemed in love with the guy."

Liv scoffed. "Are you serious? Tons of people kill people they're in love with. I mean, he was married, right? To someone other than Fergie? I'd say if she was in love with him, that's even more reason to kill him."

"Not anymore," I said, shaking my head. "Dr. C's wife died about six months ago. Cancer. Fergie told me."

My brain zoomed in on the memory of my talk with Fergie in her office when she'd mentioned having a history with Dr. Campbell. Had she said they were an item off and on? How long had they been off if his wife had died six months ago?

What if this was some kind of jealous revenge from a decidedly dramatic scorned lover? Was it possible my favorite teacher *could've* done this?

Not privy to my frantic thoughts, Liv "hmmm"ed for a moment, then said, "Yeah, I suppose that weakens the motive. What about Stephanie?"

I waved a hand, shaking my head. "It was her mother who died, since Dr. C was her stepdad. She had a good, friendly relationship with him, though, so I really don't see a motive there."

Liv nodded. "Why would she kill another parent after

recently losing one?" She stared at her list a little longer. "So it looks like Evilsworth is our best guess at this point."

I gulped down my worries about Fergie.

"Nancy would find out if he had the opportunity and a weapon next." I pointed to the pad of paper.

"So if he wasn't killed by the pills, how *did* he die?" Liv asked.

"I think he was poisoned."

"Very Shakespeare." Liv clicked her tongue.

I nodded. "Which fits with the quotes from the different plays."

"But Evilsworth hates Shakespeare. Why would he quote The Bard?"

"Exactly. No one would suspect him." I chewed on my bottom lip. "Plus, that would make sense. Only someone who didn't care about Shakespeare or wasn't well versed in it would get that line wrong."

Liv sighed. "Okay. I guess the next step would be to find out where he was right before you found the body."

Nodding, I realized I was actually looking forward to Evilsworth's class tomorrow.

9

Normally, on the days I had Evilsworth's class, my shoulders grew tenser the closer I got to setting foot in the classroom. But that afternoon, I had an excited skip to my step and couldn't wait to take my seat in his stuffy, creativity-stifling classroom. I was even early, something I'd not been since the very first day of my freshman year.

The door opened and I nearly shivered with anticipation as Evilsworth strode into the room. *Could I get him to confess? Could I trip him up and make him spill the whole thing to me like villains did in movies?* Murderers were always waiting for a chance to tell someone about the exact way they killed someone... right?

"Let's get started," Evilsworth's low voice boomed around the room as he towered over us.

I hated how he used his size to intimidate people. I mean, the man had to be close to six foot seven, the only hair left on his head was concentrated into two dark, furrowed eyebrows, and his hands were so big he could probably palm the bottom of a gallon of milk without stretching a finger. Come to think of it, they were the perfect mitts for wrapping around some unsuspecting person's throat and squeezing—tight.

I shook my head. No. Dr. Campbell hadn't been strangled. My eyes narrowed and my lips curled into a grin. Ahh, yet another way to throw the police off his scent. Smart man. *Shakespeare at the crime scene? Why, I hate Shakespeare! Poison, you say? I could've squashed the man's skull with one hand. Why in the world would I have poisoned him?* Luckily, I saw through such obfuscation.

After listening to the man drone on about Steinbeck for the better part of the hour—even though the course was Literary Criticism and Theory, not American Literature, the man had a way of working in Steinbeck wherever he could—he finally let us go for the day. I bit my bottom lip as I packed up my things. Holding my fat textbook in front of me since it wouldn't quite squeeze into my already-full messenger bag, I walked up to the front of the room. My fingers gripped the edges of the book like a shield.

"Excuse me, Professor." I cleared my throat.

The man's face tightened, the muscles in his jaw taut as he looked down on me. "Ms. Brooks, what is it?"

"Um…" The word echoed in the now-empty room. Suddenly, confronting a possible murderer seemed like a terrible idea.

He leaned forward. I took a step back.

"I was thinking of doing my paper on the theory Steinbeck's writing was directly influenced by Shakespeare."

Evilsworth pulled in a deep, tortured breath. "And what similarities, besides sharing the initial consonant in their surnames, could you possibly think would show that?" His normally pink head almost glowed red.

I blinked. "There are marked similarities between Lady

Macbeth and Curley's wife in *Of Mice and Men* and I was thinking—"

"Ms. Brooks, there is about as much evidence of that as there is Hemingway was writing about his cats instead of love and war."

Which was false—the evidence part, not the thing about the cats—because I'd finished my paper last night and had found plenty of evidence. I swallowed and tried to delicately sidestep his comment.

"I'm not the only one who thought so. I heard Dr. Campbell was going to talk about something similar in his lecture and I was really looking forward to it." Okay, that was a lie, but one I needed to bring the late professor into the conversation.

Evilsworth's spine straightened.

"He sounded like such a brilliant man. Did you get a chance to talk with him before he… died?"

"I—um—we chatted briefly, yes." He dipped his head in a stiff nod. "Excuse me, Pepper, I need to—go," he stammered and then spun out of the room.

My mouth hung open in surprise.

"Why do you do it, Pepper?" A voice asked from behind me.

Whirling around, I saw the tall, lumpy form of Destiny, Evilsworth's TA. The girl was actually quite thin, but whether from ill-fitting clothing or her interesting physique, she always seemed to bulge under and out of her clothes.

I cleared my throat. "Do what, exactly?"

"Writing term papers on topics you know he'll hate. He's going to count you down for ineffective evidence." She rolled her eyes.

"Actually, I believe it's you who does most of the grading, isn't it?"

Her eyes shifted to the floor for a moment. "He checks over them."

In the elite and cutthroat world of English department TAs, I was somewhat infamous. While I wasn't *technically* a TA in the sense I would teach classes and grade papers, I helped Fergie out where I could. This usually meant tackling mundane tasks, ones that *should* make me want to shout with boredom. But with her by my side we always managed to get deep into a conversation until, eventually, we would move to the small couch outside her office, chatting and sipping on tea.

I took this chance to see if I could catch Destiny off guard.

"Where was Evensworth on Tuesday night between six and seven?" I watched her face like Hammy watched mine whenever I ate.

Her features froze. "Pepper, do you promise not to tell anyone?" She rushed forward, linking her arm through mine and pulling me close, her eyes slid across the empty room and landed on the door.

Gulping, I nodded. "Of course."

"Tuesday night, Dr. Evensworth was in a terrible rage over what Dr. Campbell had written about his book." Her eyes were wide and rimmed in white, her nostrils flared. "He was pacing in his office, knocking things over right and left, and then…" She glanced to the door again.

"And then…?" I prompted, heart pounding, head light.

"He punched the wall and said he was going to find that little British man and show him what 'unsubstantiated drivel' *he* was. I followed him, afraid he was going to hurt someone, but he didn't seem to care if there was a witness. We found the professor in Dr. Ferguson's office and he grabbed the poor guy's neck then started squeezing."

My thoughts raced as Destiny let go of my arm... *But I hadn't seen any marks on Dr. C's neck...* My eyes shifted to the ceiling as I thought through the evidence. It didn't make sense. I looked back at Destiny, a million questions on my lips, and I caught the ill-intent shimmering in her eyes.

Oh. Destiny was messing with me. I should've expected as much from a person who would willingly spend more time than they had to with Evilsworth.

"Haha. Okay, thanks for nothing." I headed for the door, shaking my head.

Destiny broke into a fit of snorting giggles. "Oh, Pepper. That was—hehe—you should've seen—ha—I've never had so much—"

I didn't wait to hear the rest, letting the door close behind me.

MY SISTER, Maggie, snorted out a giggle in the same annoying way when I told her the story later that day.

"Oh, Peps," Maggie said, covering her mouth with her hand, as if it might hide the laughter.

I sighed. "I know it's Evilsworth. I just need the proof."

She quirked an eyebrow at me. Maggie always had big-sister advice in her back pocket, ready to help me see my misguided ways.

"I can't imagine why you thought it would be as easy as asking his TA."

"I know." Little sister, little voice.

"Was the fight real or did she make that up, too?" Maggie placed her hands on her lower back and arched her spine, grimacing at the weight of her pregnant belly.

"That's the thing. I don't know. I heard about the fight from some of my classmates at the library, too."

Maggie leaned forward and tapped her fingers on the granite countertops of her immaculate kitchen.

"Were they there?" Maggie asked.

"No. They'd only heard about the fight."

Josh, my brother-in-law, walked into the room as I said that, carrying Brooklyn over his shoulder while she squirmed and squealed. His eyebrows lifted at the word "fight."

"I don't care what they're saying, Danny didn't do it." Josh put Brooklyn down, tickling her as she raced over to me. Even through the playful gesture, Josh's face remained serious.

Maggie and I glanced at each other.

"Do what?" I asked warily as Brooklyn ran off into the other room.

"You're talking about the professor who died, right?" Josh worked in the IT department of the university, so even though he wasn't a Pine Crest native, he still stayed pretty up-to-date on the local happenings.

I nodded.

"I know it wasn't Danny," he said again.

"Danny? As in the guy you hired despite the multiple assault charges on his record?" Maggie asked.

Josh rolled his eyes. "Yeah, that one. He's also my best technician and is really trying to turn things around. He didn't kill the guy."

Maggie threw up a hand. "Who said he did?"

Josh's face wrinkled in confusion. "Pepper just did."

Maggie and I shook our heads slowly.

I pulled in a quick breath. "Wait, Dr. C got in *another* fight right before he died?"

"Another?" Josh scowled.

"I wasn't talking about Danny just now. Apparently Evilsworth also had it out with the man right before he wound up dead," I explained. "And you said you know he didn't do it. How?" I looked at my brother-in-law.

Josh said, "Danny's got a hot temper, but who could blame him? That Campbell wouldn't shut up about the sound until Danny blew up at him, but that's all it was, a fight."

"Were you with him the whole time?" I tried to picture who Danny was. I think he'd helped Fergie the other day when her speakers went out. Big guy. Scruffy. A little rough.

"No, he took a smoke break right after the fight, saying he needed to calm down a bit before the lecture started or…" Josh stopped, swallowing hard.

"Or what?" Maggie asked, hand on her hip.

"Or he was going to punch that damn doctor in the face the next time he saw him." Creases formed on Josh's forehead as he realized how incriminating it sounded.

I tapped the pen on the counter. "And how long was this smoke break?"

Josh shrugged. "I dunno, like ten minutes. He came back and got to work, but then we heard the news and—well—realized we no longer needed to set up for the lecture, so we made sure there wasn't anything we could do to help and went home."

My toes curled in my shoes as I thought. This was good information, but it didn't make sense. Why would some random sound guy kill him after one fight, and why would he leave a Shakespeare quote behind?

"Have you ever seen Danny and Fergie together?" I asked, thinking of the second note, the one I'd found in her purse.

Josh nodded. "Yeah. He likes her. Thinks she's hilarious."

I smooshed my lips together. "I think you might be right, Josh. It doesn't sound like Danny had enough of a motive to kill Dr. Campbell."

"Right?" His shoulders relaxed as I said this.

By the time I left that night after dinner, I knew two things: I may not think Danny did it, but I was definitely adding him to the suspect list. Also, I needed to talk to the person my classmates claimed had told them about the fight between Evilsworth and Campbell. Maybe she'd seen something that could break this case wide open.

10

The next day, I waited in the hall so I could question Trish and Heather about this "Katie" person they'd mentioned. I leaned against the wall as I watched the students walk by me.

As I stood there like a creepy stalker, I mused about how Nancy Drew stories had, in no way, prepared me for the amount of awkward waiting involved in sleuthing. I mean, reading the books it was all bravery and justice and people congratulating Nancy. But in reality, it was like ninety percent sticking your nose where it didn't belong and hoping you found something to justify the weird things you had to do to find it.

Down the hall I spotted that Danny guy Josh was talking about last night. He was exiting one of the classrooms. I chewed on my lip, knowing I should question him. My heart pounded and I moved to follow him.

Just then, Heather and Trish turned the corner, walking my way. Darn. I stopped my pursuit of Danny, unsure of which lead to follow. He quickly disappeared down another hallway, making my decision easier. I walked to Heather and

Trish, teeth bared in my friendliest, tell-me-all-the-things grin.

"Hey! So I was thinking about what you two said the other day..." I paused and looked around—no Evilsworth or Destiny to be seen—"You know, about the fight between Evensworth and Campbell."

Heather nodded. "Yeah."

I continued with my question. "Who is this Katie person you said told you about the fight? Did she see it? Could you point her out to me?"

"Don't you know Katie?" Trish asked.

Heather's forehead creased in confusion. "Yeah, Katie. In our next class. Right there." Her eyes locked on someone behind me.

Oh no. They weren't talking about—

"Katie Landin?" I asked as I turned just in time to see her change course and head over.

"Yeah! Katie." They both smiled and nodded.

I, however, stayed frozen in horror. They were right; I *did* know Katie Landin. She'd been in the same hall as me in the dorms. By the second week of school our freshman year, I'd nicknamed her Crazy Katie because of all of the wacky things she always said. Katie was the kind of crazy that was downright exhausting.

In fact, as she pranced up to us with wide eyes and red lipstick a few shades too bright, I felt my shoulders preemptively slump from fatigue.

"Hey-hey-hey!" she said and then cackled out a loud laugh.

I gritted my teeth. "Hi, Katie."

"Pepper! I see you all the time but we never get the chance to chat." She gave my arm an unsolicited squeeze.

Yeah, I thought. *That's more than a coincidence.*

"I know! This quarter's been crazy-busy for everyone," I said.

Heather and Trish backed me up with supportive nods.

"Omigosh, the funniest thing happened the other day, Pepper! I ran into Michael."

Michael was my latest boyfriend, the one who'd broken my heart last summer when he moved to Seattle to start his career.

"Oh," I squeaked out.

Katie said, "Yeah, I was visiting my cousin in the city and bumped into him. He was with some model-looking girl who looked like she'd just jumped out of a J. Crew shoot."

Just what everyone loved to hear, right?

"Didn't stop him from perusing the goods, though," Katie added, clicking her tongue as she motioned to her body.

I almost groaned. Katie constantly thought guys were hitting on her; it didn't matter whether they were way older or way younger than her, she was going to tell you they were totally "all over" her. And even though I was pretty sure Michael hadn't been blatantly "perusing the goods," I added it to the list of things I didn't want to hear about my ex.

Heather cleared her throat. "Well... we've got—"

Trish nodded. "Yeah..."

They turned on their heels and headed into class, leaving me as a sacrifice with only a quick glance behind them.

"I mean, was he like that when he was with you?" Katie asked, bringing me back into a conversation I was so desperately wishing I could escape.

I shook my head. No, and that was the problem. Michael had been great, almost perfect. I mean, the guy was a little too in love with the gym and had this annoying obsession with "clean eating"—he'd never said anything, but I could feel his frustration at how I spent most of my time curled up on couches reading and eating carbs.

I had stupidly thought we had a future together, even believed him when he said he wanted to stay here with me. But after graduation, he'd called it off and left anyway, saying this town was too small for him. Small or not, Pine Crest was in my bones. I didn't want to leave it, not ever. That's when I'd decided to stop dating guys from NWU.

Katie continued to prattle on about her run-in with Michael.

"... I mean, you would think some woman who could've easily been a model could hold a man's attention, but it's not the case. I see it all the time. A lot of guys think they want someone who's stick thin, but they can't seem to keep their eyes off all of this." Katie laughed and swung her hips as she gestured to her body.

And just like that, my hopes of clearing Fergie's name sank to the speckled Berber carpet of the hallway. I couldn't trust the word of a person for whom making stuff up was as natural as breathing. For all I knew, based on how Katie twisted completely normal interactions, Evilsworth and Campbell could've simply passed by each other in the hall without saying hello and Katie perceived it as a huge fight.

Despite the gloom settling over me, I faked a laugh to show Katie that yes, I agreed she had it "goin' on" for sure.

"Well... good talking to you," I said, and moved in the direction Trish and Heather had gone. "See you around."

Once in class, I slumped into my seat. Evilsworth strode into the room. Not only had I found out Crazy Katie was the witness I'd been so excited about, but I'd also missed my chance to talk to Danny. Crossing my arms over my chest, I decided today was officially the worst.

By the time class was over that afternoon, the only possible thing that could save me from the foul mood I'd gotten myself into was to spend some time in my favorite spot on campus—besides the library, that is. My spot was just behind the science building, next to the creek. There was a small bench next to an old willow tree. Between the babbling water and the way the wind would whip around the side of the building to rustle the willows long, leafy branches, it was by far the most relaxing place on campus. I had a book I'd been meaning to start and an hour to kill before I needed to head home and let Hammy out.

My feet began to take me there as if they were a horse who knew the way back to the barn by heart. As I walked, I went over the facts of the case in my head.

Motive-wise, both Evilsworth and this Danny character had reason to harm the doctor, though Danny's was much less convincing than Evilsworth's. But Josh had said he had a history of violence, so... Who was I to say what might set someone off? I mean, I was known to get irrationally angry when someone bought the last scone in front of me in line at Bittersweet, and I didn't even have an anger management problem.

I tried to be objective and think about Fergie and any possible motives she might have to off her former lover. I supposed the fact they used to be involved brought another level of depth to their relationship, and depth was ripe for hiding all manner of strife—if reading the classics had taught me anything. Fergie mentioning how they'd been involved "off and on" definitely added a new layer of questions to this conundrum, but I still felt sure my mentor couldn't have killed the man.

Opportunity, it seemed, favored all three suspects. Fergie knew Dr. C was in her office and had been slightly flustered when I'd seen her walking away from the place, but she had been with Stephanie. Evilsworth could've been in the building at that time, though I still needed to verify all of this since he had all but run away yesterday when I tried to ask him about the deceased doctor—yet another tidbit that made him seem less than innocent, I might add. And Danny, as Josh had reluctantly shared, had been on a smoke break during the exact time the doctor had been offed.

It was the weapon that had me the most stumped, however. I mean, poison? Who used poison these days? That part definitely fit the Shakespeare quotes. When they weren't stabbing each other in the back, or beheading each other, the characters in Shakespeare's plays did seem to favor poison. But who could even get their hands on the stuff these days?

Without access to the police database, without knowledge of what kind of poison had killed the guy, I was decidedly up a creek in this investigation. In real life, however, I was now standing beside a creek, having finally reached my destination. The fresh, crisp air wafting up off the water mixed with the quiet babbling of the creek over gray and blue-toned rocks. I shook my head and felt the weight of all of this on my shoulders, and I was looking forward to sitting down in silence and letting it all slip away with the breeze.

That was when I noticed someone already sitting in my favorite spot. Just as quickly, my brain recognized the dark hair.

Alex.

Ugh. I really did just want to be alone. But I wasn't about to let him kick me out of my favorite spot. So I walked over anyway, pulling my bag off my shoulder and scooting onto the bench next to him.

Alex's attention jumped from his book to me. "Hey."

"Come here often?"

"Sometimes."

"Huh. Me, too." I pulled my book from my bag and opened it with every intention of losing myself in my reading.

I thought I could feel his eyes on me, watching me warily for a few seconds before going back to his book. But even when he seemed to be reading, too, I couldn't focus. I suddenly wanted to know what he was reading. My gaze tiptoed over his shoulder and my breath caught in my throat.

The man was reading Dickens. *A Tale of Two Cities* to be exact. I emitted a small "eeee" sound before I could stop myself. I saw Alex's lip twitch, but he didn't look in my direction. Dickens was my absolute, hands-down, fan-girl-status, favorite author. I loved him like Fergie loved The Bard.

My lips pressed tightly together, as if that might keep the words from spilling out. But after the span of two breaths, I couldn't hold them in any longer.

"That's one of my favorite books. What part are you at?"

Alex sighed and let the book rest in his lap. "Um... there was a whole bunch of wine in the street, some guy delivered a letter, and now they're talking with some crazy old guy who lives in an attic and makes shoes."

I scoffed. "That crazy old guy is Lucie's father. She thought he was dead."

"Yeah, but I'm on page..." he checked, "fifty and pretty much nothing's happened yet."

"Just wait," I said. "The ending is *so* worth it."

Alex raised his eyebrows in an okay-sure-but-I'm-not-getting-my-hopes-up kind of way.

"I'm serious, it's lovely and heartbreaking and you won't be able to read it without crying." I remembered staying up until two in the morning to finish the last few pages and how tears had streamed down my face when I flipped to the back cover.

Alex said, "So if he can write an ending that good, why couldn't he make the rest of this stuff more interesting? Why wait to give us the good stuff until the end?"

"The ending means nothing if you don't get to know the characters. The less interesting part is character building."

He wrinkled his forehead. "A hundred or so pages of getting to know people? Seems like overkill. Take Melville, for instance. 'Call me Ishmael.' First line. Alright. Got it. This guy is Ishmael. Next few lines, I find out he's poor and he's a sailor. Cool, I care about him and now the good stuff can start to happen."

My head fell back and a groan escaped me. "You've got to be kidding me. One paragraph and you're good?" Before he could answer, I pointed at him and added, "And don't try to tell me your guy Melville didn't drone on with the best of them. I definitely fell asleep more than once while I was reading that *whale* of a novel."

He ignored my cut to Melville—and my awesome pun—and said, "I guess I've always been able to make my mind up about people pretty quick. I don't need more than a few minutes in real life."

"Really?" I asked, incredulous.

His dark brown eyes snapped onto mine like our pupils were constructed out of the opposite poles of two magnets.

"Yeah. Like when I first met you." He stared at me and I could feel my cheeks heat up under his gaze.

It was the first time he'd treated me like anything other than an inconvenience, annoyingly always where I shouldn't be. I suddenly worried I might not be ready to hear what he thought of me and my eyes angled down, focusing on my hands instead.

"I knew you were going to be trouble."

"Trouble?" I asked, waiting for yet another *hilarious* mention of how I'd almost sabotaged his father's investigation. But when I met his eyes again, the softness behind them made me falter. My mouth gaped open for a second before I clamped it shut.

Alex nodded. "The first day I saw you, you were wearing some huge gray sweater my grandpa would've worn, and it was eighty degrees outside."

I squirmed. I hadn't worn that gray sweater for months, having forgotten it over at Maggie's. Which meant he'd noticed me back during the summer.

Clearing my throat, I said, "Wool is very breathable and can keep you cool, especially in humid climates." My words were small and sounded like whispers after his deep ones.

"You strode into that library like you owned the place, plopped your stuff down on the chair, kicked off your shoes, and tucked your feet under you as you sank into the cushion."

I *was* pretty cocky when it came to my library.

"Did you know you move your toes when you read?" he asked, moving slightly closer.

I nodded, glancing at his lips and then down at my lap. I could almost feel Alex's gaze on my face, studying me. He leaned forward.

At that point in my life, I'd kissed a good handful of

guys. Some had been great, some not so much. I wasn't an expert by any measure, but I knew enough to recognize what was happening. Alex was going to kiss me.

I licked my lips and… blurted out the first thing that came to my mind. "I know who killed Dr. Campbell."

11

Of course, I didn't *actually* know who had killed Dr. C. So when Alex sat back and spat out, "What?" my eyes swiveled about.

Alex, however, patiently waited for me to answer his question that hung between us. Not that there was all that much space between us; he was still sitting very close.

Besides the initial and most obvious flaw in my statement—that I couldn't definitively name the killer—Alex's furrowed brow brought to mind another important consideration that had been overlooked when my brain was grabbing the idea from the pile marked "quick fixes." Alex had told me to stay out of the investigation and the fact I wasn't heeding his advice was supposed to be a secret, from him especially.

"Pepper," he said in a low growl, his eyes darkening.

Biting my lip, I thought up a few more reactive, and equally terrible, ideas. After going through each of them, I decided running away was my only remaining course of action. My body lurched forward.

"Freeze," he said in his best, commanding police officer

tone. His voice cut through me and I did, in some sort of awkward squat position. "Sit back down."

I sucked in a deep breath and plopped my butt onto the bench, again. "Okay," I groaned. "You got me. I don't actually know who did it." I paused. "Hey, I'm considering getting a part-time job. Do you think you could put a good word in for me at the library?" I willed him to go along with the change in subject.

He cocked one eyebrow, ignored my attempted diversion, and said, "I thought you were going to let this go."

Despite how the man all but screamed skeptical vibes, there was something about those dark brown eyes and his charming complete disregard of charm, that made me inherently trust him.

"I'm still looking into the case. But only because I've gotten a few leads and I have to clear Fergie's name."

"Leads?" he asked.

"Dr. Campbell got in two fights right before he died. One with some sound guy and the other with one of my teachers, who is an *awful* person, by the way. I'm pretty sure that teacher is the one who did it. I just don't have any—you know—evidence to actually prove that."

Alex chuckled. "Yeah, that pesky evidence gets in the way all the time."

I huffed. "I'm working on it. I found a witness, but I'm not quite sure if she's reliable."

Alex's forehead furrowed as he seemed to digest this news. Seconds later, his attention settled back on me. His face softened and he leaned toward me again, his hand moving to cup my cheek.

Wait. How'd we get back to kissing?

I panicked, but this time refrained from blurting out random exclamations—mostly because they had proven to be an impermanent solution to the problem, but also because I realized I kinda *wanted* to kiss Alex. I could smell his minty breath and feel the warmth of his hand.

Just about to let my eyelids flutter closed and give in to his probably devastatingly soft lips, I watched his fingers curl and then pluck something from my hair. My skin flushed hot and cold as I focused on the crispy fall leaf he pulled from my hair and held up for me to see. He leaned back, dropping the leaf to the ground.

Dear lord. The man hadn't been about to kiss me after all. My mind reeled. *Had I leaned in? Could he tell I thought it was a kiss?*

Alex stood up. "I could go with you. Give you a second opinion about the witness." He folded down one of the pages of his book, and then shut it.

It took me a moment to let go of my pride, but eventually my rational brain won out. The truth was, it would be nice to have someone with police training there with me. Heck, I hadn't actually questioned Katie earlier. I should at least give her a chance.

"Okay... but I've gotta warn you, she's a complete flirt, all over any guy she sees."

His mouth pulled into a smirk. "I think I can handle it."

A shiver danced up my spine. I blinked, getting my thoughts straight. He was absolutely the kind of guy I didn't want to find myself falling for: a university student, a book strangler, seemingly mad at the world, and on his way out of town after graduation.

You wanted him to kiss you, though. What was that about? My unhelpful mind chose this moment to be coherent enough to analyze the situation.

I haven't kissed anyone in a while and I got confused...

"You coming?" Alex asked as he started walking up the

small slope to the concrete path. I grabbed my bag and followed the guy, repeating affirmations in my head as I did.

Alex wasn't about to kiss me.
And I wouldn't have wanted him to, if he had been.
Which he wasn't.
Because he finds me annoying.
As I do him.
And gruff... brusque... ill-tempered... churlish.

A peace settled over me as I returned to my love of vocabulary, a mental sanctuary in my time of need.

Our shoes scraped and crunched across the concrete pathway that snaked through campus. Pulling my jacket tighter, I gestured to a walkway that would take us to the cafeteria where Katie worked. She normally covered dinner hours. I knew because I avoided the building during those times so I wouldn't run into her. The sun was setting, as it was late fall in the northwest which meant sunsets at dinnertime. Bright oranges and pinks splashed the sky, making the campus look like it was being shot through one of those perfume-commercial filters, soft and dreamy. I peeked at Alex. His face was tipped up as he took in the same beautiful, slow-burning sky.

"It's really pretty around here," he said, after a moment.

I nodded. "Where are you from originally?" I asked.

"California."

"Do you miss it?" I watched him.

He sighed, then shook his head. "It's a different kind of beauty down there, but it also holds a few too many painful memories for me to appreciate it. At least for now."

That was when I remembered the "was" he'd used the other day when talking about his mom. And this new mention of pain only added to my list of evidence she had, in fact, passed away.

Swallowing, I curled my fingers into fists. I got the pain Alex was talking about, even though he didn't know how well I could relate.

The lights of the dining hall shone brightly in front of us as we came to the end of the path. A grassy hill was dotted with laughing students, hanging out on the cool lawn after dinner. We reached the large double doors of the dining hall and Alex held one open for me.

Once inside, I led the way to a table by the window where I spotted Katie cleaning up trays of dishes the diners had left behind. There were only a few students eating and the place was fairly quiet. We must've just missed the big rush. Katie's long blond hair was piled on top of her head in a messy bun and her apron was spotted with food stains.

Glancing up as we approached, Katie's face lit up.

"Oh, hey Pepper!" She smiled, placing the tray of dishes on the nearest table. Her eyes landed on Alex behind me and I could see her blue eyes focus in on him, like lasers, ignoring me after that. "And who do we have here?"

Alex held his right hand out to shake hers. At the same time he wrapped his left arm around my shoulders.

"Hey, I'm Alex."

I tensed up when he squeezed me close. Okay, vocabulary was definitely not going to help me out of this one. Mostly because the only words coming to mind were ones like *solid*, *strong*, and *handsome*.

Like me, Katie seemed to be going through her own list of adjectives. She blushed as she shook his hand. Her focus moved to Alex's arm wrapped around me. The guy was clutching me to him like a signed first edition at a used book sale.

"Pepper, you didn't tell me you were seeing someone new." She let go of his hand. "I was telling you all about seeing Michael yesterday and you didn't even hint you'd moved on."

"Oh, I—uh—" I stammered, looking at Alex for help.

"It's pretty recent," Alex said. He snaked his other arm around my waist and pulled me closer, looking at me like Liv and I look at chocolate during finals week, like we look at coffee after late nights studying.

"Extremely," I croaked out.

Katie's eyes played Follow the Leader with Alex's hands. Finally, they snapped back to my face. "What are you doing here? I thought you and Liv got a place off campus."

I hadn't eaten a meal at the dining hall in two years, actually. But I couldn't seem to answer or get my brain to focus on the questions I'd needed to ask her. It was too busy cataloging everywhere Alex was touching me: *stomach, waist, shoulder, lower back, rib*s. My thoughts were officially thirteen all over again, giggly and crushing hard. If I'd had any Lisa Frank stationary, his name would've been scribbled all over it, complete with hearts and "4EVAs."

"Mi pimienta, didn't you have something you wanted to ask?" Alex gestured toward Katie, as if he knew I'd forgotten she was there.

And now a sweet nickname, too? I had no clue what it meant, but that didn't stop me from almost melting to the floor. Alex held me up.

I cleared my throat. "Oh, right. Uh, Katie, Trish and Heather told me you saw Evensworth fighting with Dr. Campbell the other day, before he…" my voice cut out.

Katie nodded. "Yeah, they were yelling at each other in the hallway and I turned the corner and stumbled into the middle of it. But I turned and left right away. They looked pretty mad."

"You left right away? You didn't hear anything they

said?" Alex asked, his sweet, fake boyfriend persona replaced by his police officer training.

Katie shook her head. "I heard Evensworth yell how Dr. Campbell wasn't going to get away with this and then they stopped yelling when I walked up. That's all I heard."

If I had actually thought Katie could've given me important information about the case, this might've been a devastating blow to my investigation. But I had been expecting this to be a dead end.

"You don't think...?" Katie glanced down at her shoes for a moment and then back up at us.

"No. Just asking around," Alex said and I could feel his body shift, ready to leave.

"I hope they catch the killer." Katie shivered. "Sorry I didn't hear more." Her eyes lit up as she said this and then she added, "Hey, there was another lady in the hall with me. I think she heard a lot more of the argument. You should ask her."

Alex and I straightened. "Who?" I asked.

"I didn't recognize her," Katie said. "She was tiny and had blond hair, looked like a little bird hiding behind Dr. Campbell."

Eyes wide, I whispered, "Stephanie."

12

At this newest piece of information, Alex's arm tightened around me, in what seemed like an uncharacteristic physical expression of excitement.

"Nice meeting you, Katie," he called over his shoulder as he maneuvered me out of the dining hall.

Between the shock of having Alex's grabby hands all over me and the clue Katie had given us, I was mostly a marionette puppet, at that point. Alex had to pretty much carry me out of there.

Outside, Alex's arm promptly left my body, the ruse officially at an end. I tugged at my light jacket and stepped away from him.

He winked. "Told you I could handle it."

"Yeah." The word came out breathier than I wanted. I cleared my throat. "I don't see why you couldn't have warned me you were going to get all handsy."

"And miss the look on your face? Naw, that was priceless." He chuckled.

"Rude," I muttered. Luckily, the tip we'd learned from Katie had my head buzzing with more than just my frustration with Alex. "So if Stephanie saw the fight, too," I thought aloud, "she might be able to tell us more about what happened next."

He nodded. "So where to?"

I motioned to my right with a jerk of my head. "The Pine Crest Inn," I answered cheerfully.

"You heard she was staying there?"

After a quick shrug, I said, "Not really, it's just where everyone stays."

"Wouldn't the university put them up in one of the dorms?"

"Not when you've got the beautiful and relaxing Pine Crest Inn in which to house guests."

Alex chuckled and we walked toward Main Street, which acted as a border between the campus and the downtown section of Pine Crest. It was getting darker as the minutes ticked by. The streetlights of the university flicked on above us as we walked and I was secretly happy to have Alex along. Up until now, I'd always felt safe on campus and in our little town. But tonight, I felt the unmistakable tingle of fear distorting normal sights and sounds.

"You really don't have to come with me, you know. I could do this on my own," I said, just making sure.

Alex dipped his head. "True, but I'm pretty sure your favorite professor is the killer, so I'd rather not leave you alone if it's all the same to you."

His words took me by surprise. I knew his dad suspected Fergie, but... "You said she might be in danger. She—someone left her that note as a threat." Frustration tightened my chest.

He opened his palms. "That was before I learned more about the case. Look, I don't want it to be true, but right now I haven't heard anything to convince me otherwise. He was found in her office, no one can substantiate her claim she was 'running around to prepare for the lecture.' They have a romantic past, a note with the same handwriting was later found in her purse, and the poison used to kill Dr. Campbell sounds eerily similar to the one in Hamlet." Alex paced while he rattled off the evidence.

My brain switched gears from frustration to interest as he confirmed my suspicions about the poison.

"Wait, he was for sure poisoned then?"

Alex's face fell for a moment. He obviously wasn't supposed to tell me that. With a sigh, he said, "Yes, but please don't tell anyone, Pepper. This is an active investigation."

I nodded, scrunching my forehead tight as I digested the new information. I mean, not *new* necessarily, but hearing it confirmed by Alex made more difference than I thought it would.

"It's the same poison from Hamlet, then?" I asked, trying to remember the name of that deadly elixir. I was no Fergie, so it took me a few seconds to locate the place where the name sat in my brain. "Hebanon? But it's not real. He made it up."

Pressing his lips together—maybe because he'd already told me too much and needed a physical reminder to keep his mouth shut—Alex nodded. "The poison that killed the professor is one of the few they think Shakespeare meant, based on how it was administered and how quickly it killed the king."

Contemplating where one might get such a poison around Pine Crest, I turned toward the inn. Alex kept pace next to me as I started walking again.

"I'm still kinda mad at you for thinking it's Fergie," I mumbled after a few blocks.

"I can live with that," Alex replied.

We walked in silence the rest of the way. As we approached the inn, the yellow streetlights were replaced by the crisp, white shine from outdoor strings of Edison bulbs. They were strung together on the wisteria-covered lattice of the front trellis-framed entry.

"Beautiful and relaxing." Alex dipped his chin in appreciation.

Pulling open the large wood and glass front door, I led the way inside.

Betsy, a friend of my mom's and the manager of the inn, sat behind the front desk. Her graying hair was pulled into a tight ponytail and she seemed wide awake despite the fact we were creeping steadily toward the "sober-suited matron" of the night.

"Oh my goodness," she crooned. "Aren't you a sight, Pepper. I haven't seen you since…" Betsy stopped at that point, realizing—as I already had—that the last time we saw each other was at my dad's funeral almost a year ago.

I studied the ceiling, because it had beautiful dark wood beams running across it and not at all because it kept the tears crowding my eyes at bay.

After a moment and a deep breath, I glanced back toward Betsy. The woman's rosy cheeks pressed up into a knowing smile. Her blue eyes appeared to be suffering from the same inconvenient level of moisture as mine.

"What can I do for you two?" Betsy asked, her smile faltering a little as she glanced at Alex.

"Dr. Davis Campbell's daughter, Stephanie; is she here?" I asked.

Betsy shook her head. "No, she's still out." The woman craned her neck to peek at the clock positioned on the wall.

"But she's been getting back around this time each night if you want to wait." She motioned to a few chairs in the foyer. I nodded. "Thanks."

We turned to sit on the plush couches lining the waiting area of the inn. I ducked out from under the strap of my messenger bag and propped it next to the couch.

If anyone asked, I would tell them I was slightly annoyed when Alex plopped down next to me instead of occupying the second couch. In reality, however, the weight of his body next to mine and the fresh laundry smell he toted around with him like a bent-up paperback in his pocket were both welcome comforts after the kick of emotion I'd just received.

Out of the corner of my eye, I could see Alex studying me. His eyes flicking between me and the main counter where Betsy had gotten back to work. He hadn't missed the awkward, sad air that had gathered between us for those moments, or the redness which I'm sure still rimmed my eyes. I could almost hear the questions lining up in his mind.

His chance to move the question queue forward came a few moments later when Betsy excused herself to go check on a guest.

"Did you bury her dog the last time you saw each other or something?" Alex asked when we were alone.

"My dad, actually."

I wanted to close my eyes as the words left me, but I looked at my sneakers instead. They were smudged and dirty compared to the pristine wood floors and expensive wool rugs of the inn.

After a silent moment, I dug deep and finally muscled a glance up to gauge the impact of my words. The man sitting next to me was tense, all clenched jaw muscles and wrinkled brow. He stared at the front door of the inn as if he were looking through it, past it, possibly all the way down to California.

My stomach dropped. Crap. I'd forgotten about his mom. This time I did close my eyes and used the painful silence to berate myself for, yet again, blurting out something I should've kept to myself.

A hand settled over mine, squeezing tight and my eyes flew open. While Alex's face hadn't let go of any of the tightness, his brown eyes were gentle as they watched me.

"I'm so sorry. How? When?"

"Almost a year. Heart attack." My voice sounded gravelly, foreign, not my own. "And your mom?" I asked in the stranger's voice.

He glanced away quickly, but the flash of pain I caught behind those brown eyes made my stomach churn.

"She was shot." His voice broke around the words and the hand holding mine tightened.

Shot. The word made my mouth feel dry. I had a million questions, but kept quiet as I studied his face and saw he had more to say.

"In California, where we used to live. My dad and I moved up here a few months after it happened, needing to get away. Dad wanted to be in a smaller town where things weren't so dangerous. Our neighborhood back home was pretty heavy with crime, gangs, that sort of thing."

So that was why the Valdez men were so cold, so serious.

Alex swallowed and turned toward me. "It's been six months. Does it ever get better?"

Pulling in a deep breath, I said, "Sort of. It gets less… stabby feeling, if that makes sense. There was a long time where every time I remembered he was gone, it would be like someone had stuck a kitchen knife into my stomach. It still hurts, but it's more of a sting instead, and other days just a dull ache."

He smiled and I decided—never having seen his father recreate such an expression—this light and wonderful gesture was something he'd inherited from his mother. While this didn't erase my anger at him completely, I would be lying if I said it hadn't lessened it, a lot. I met his smile with a hopeful one of my own.

In the midst of our moment, Betsy returned to her desk, her eyes tracking us in our close, hands-clasped-tight state as she clicked around on her computer. My cheeks heated up and I snuck my hand away from his.

Just as I was feeling like I might be digging myself out of the sadness that had piled over us during our conversation, the most recent victim of a deceased parent walked in through the inn's front door.

13

My first reaction, upon seeing Stephanie, was to run up to her and envelop her in a we-know-your-pain, Kumbaya, children-of-dead-parents-club hug. Luckily, I was learning to think before I spoke, or acted. Plus, Alex beat me to it. His greeting was decidedly less emotionally charged.

"Stephanie," he said matter-of-factly as he stood.

The small woman was even thinner, more washed out than last time I'd seen her. She looked like a name penciled into the front page of a book someone had attempted to erase.

"Yes?" Her blue eyes hardened into a "who are you?" questioning stare. When she caught sight of me, however, her gaze relaxed. "Oh. Hi, Pepper"

I hadn't seen her since that night. There were so many things I wanted to say: *sorry, I know what you're going through, it'll get better.* But the only thing that came out was, "Hey."

I was actually kind of surprised the woman remembered me. But I suppose I *had* been the one to find her dad's body, so...

"I'm Alex." Alex reached forward and shook her hand. I

noticed how he didn't use his last name. I spent a few seconds wondering why until Stephanie's quiet voice broke through my conjectures.

"What can I do for the two of you?" she asked, wrapping her delicate arms around herself as the last bit of cold air from outside brushed past us.

Alex shot me a look. I got the feeling he wanted me to ask the questions. He must not have missed how her demeanor had softened when she saw me.

"We had a few questions for you about… the other day," I said.

My eyes shifted to Betsy where she sat at the front desk, doing a great job of looking busy. If I knew Betsy, though, the typing she was doing on her computer was more likely a gossipy email to the rest of Pine Crest than something for the inn.

Stephanie hesitated. Her forehead creased. "I've already told the police everything I know."

My cheeks flushed. Of course she had. Why would she tell us anything? We were just two college kids and she was the victim's stepdaughter. This was different than asking Katie a few questions in the dining hall.

I gulped, stepping close. When my dad died, I did a ton of research on the type of heart attack he'd had. I wanted to know everything about what had killed him. If Stephanie felt a similar curiosity, then maybe I could convince her to talk.

"I think the police are investigating the wrong person," I whispered in a voice low enough to ensure my words wouldn't make it into Betsy's email. Alex, however, was definitely close enough to hear.

Stephanie's face tightened and she looked to Alex as if seeking confirmation.

He sighed, but nodded. "She won't let it go."

Stephanie seemed to think for a second, but then she said, "There's a lounge next to my room and it seems pretty quiet. Would you guys like to talk there?"

"That sounds great," Alex said.

I grabbed my bag from the couch and Stephanie led the way toward the lounge. It was quiet; four chairs crowded around a gas fireplace, and a window looked out on the back gardens. We each took a seat and then the attention turned to me.

"So…?" Stephanie crossed one slender leg over the other.

"The police think Fergie did it," I blurted out.

Stephanie nodded. "I'd heard that." She folded her hands in her lap. "I can't believe it."

Leaning forward, I said, "Because it's *not* true." My fingers shook with the need for someone to believe me. I folded them in my lap.

The woman blinked at my brashness, but then she exhaled and said, "Of course it isn't. Sharon couldn't hurt a fly."

Hearing Fergie's first name caught me by surprise. But emboldened by Stephanie's support of Fergie, I plowed on with my questions.

"Stephanie, we heard you were with your father when he and Professor Evensworth got in a fight that night."

The woman swallowed as if slightly nauseated. "Stepfather. Davis was my stepfather." The whispered words left her lips and dropped like a heavy tear.

"Right." I dipped my head in acknowledgment. "Did you hear what they were fighting about?"

"Yeah. That stupid book." Stephanie's soft voice turned to ice for a second, but then recovered its normal soft British accent. "A literary journal Davis, my stepfather, often wrote reviews for, asked him to write something up for them about it."

"And did Evensworth seem mad enough to do something violent because of the review?" I asked.

Sighing, Stephanie said, "I've been asking myself that same question the last few days." She shook her head. "I don't know. He did seem incredibly angry—kept towering over us and trying to corner Davis."

That sure sounded like Evilsworth. I inwardly rolled my eyes.

"What happened after the fight?" Alex asked, his voice sounding so loud compared to Stephanie's soft tones.

"Some girl walked into the middle of it and they stopped. Not before Evensworth threatened my stepfather, telling him he 'wouldn't get away with this.' Then he stormed away and we went to check out the lecture hall. My stepfather was very particular about his microphones and wanted to make sure everything was up to his standards."

My muscles tensed as she mentioned the scene of the second fight. "You were there the whole time for that?" I asked. I could feel Alex watching me, no doubt noticing my increased interest. The fight with the sound guy had been the one thing I hadn't spilled to him about the case yet.

Stephanie nodded. "Yeah. It got pretty heated, too."

I scooted forward. "How did the sound guy seem?"

"Irrational, really. I mean, I think Davis was still kind of testy from his encounter with Evensworth, but he was only being diligent. The engineer made the fight as big as it got." Stephanie sat back in her chair and crossed her arms.

"As big?" I asked, brow furrowing.

She dipped her chin once. "Yeah, I mean, he has never

threatened to get someone sacked before. That guy was looking for a fight, though."

I glanced over at Alex. His face was unreadable—probably thanks to his police training. Trying to mirror some of his control, I pulled in a deep breath and nodded.

"Did you see that man anymore after the sound check?" Alex asked.

Stephanie shook her head. "No. We split up after that. Davis went to go look over his speech one more time and I went to see the Emily Dickinson art installation on the third floor. She was my mother's favorite poet. She passed away last year," she said, looking down at her lap.

Blinking back tears, I decided I would need more training if I wanted to have an unreadable face like Alex's. Actually, even Alex seemed to be having a tough time with this one. He cleared his throat and was really focused on a spot on his jeans for a few seconds while he recovered.

"And how long did you stay at the art exhibit?" His question surprised me when it came, as did the coldness behind his voice.

Stephanie and I both looked to Alex. His face matched his tone once again and confirmed he was, in fact, recovered from the emotions recently overcoming him and asking the woman for her alibi.

I bit my bottom lip. *I was supposed to have done that. How could I have forgotten to check something so simple?*

She blinked, only taken aback for a second before a resigned, almost thankful smile settled over her features. "I was there for about a half hour. There was a lot to see."

"Did anyone see you there?" Alex stayed on track.

"I wasn't the only one there, if that's what you mean. Sharon found me on my way back down to the first floor and then we ran into Pepper, who... knows the rest."

As her statement hit me, I heaved out a sigh. The rest. *Sure did.* Shivers skittered up and down my arms at the memory of Dr. Campbell's lifeless eyes staring back at me.

All at once, this felt like too much. The weight of the last few days crashed down on top of me. I wanted to be home, curled in my bed under multiple blankets—all the blankets. Scanning my memory for anything else we could ask and finding nothing, I stood up.

"Thanks so much for your help," I said, smiling weakly.

Stephanie nodded. "I'm just happy someone's asking about all of the suspects. I want them to find who did this more than anything."

"We're doing our best." I waved goodbye as I turned to leave.

Alex did the same and then followed me to the foyer of the inn. As we walked, that damn hand was back on my body—placed lightly on the small of my back this time. I turned to scowl it away—I really didn't want to deal with the feelings it brought up right now—but was met with the sweetest look of concern bunching up his face.

"Are you okay?" he asked, looking me up and down, as if my pain might be physical.

"Just tired. I think I need to head home."

"I'll walk you." He reached the foyer before me and opened the front door of the inn, ushering me outside.

Waving goodnight to Betsy, I stepped through the threshold. "I'm okay. I don't mind walking by myself."

I hated how much of a lie that was. I usually loved long walks alone on campus. But I couldn't seem to get rid of the vision of Dr. C's body and the knowledge his killer was still loose in Pine Crest somewhere.

Thankfully, Alex didn't pick this moment to start

listening to me. He followed as I headed toward my apartment.

The sky was a blackish blue, dotted with starry diamonds, and the smell of burning wood sat heavy in the sharp air. People were starting to build fires at night to ward off the frosty temperatures. It would be Halloween in a week. The realization would've normally made me bubble with excitement. Pine Crest during Halloween was one of my favorite things, but the murder made this year's All Hallows Eve seem too real, too eerie. A shiver raced down my back and I hugged my arms around my torso.

"Still mad at me?" Alex asked after a few moments of silence.

I puffed out a laugh, my breath forming a cloud in front of my face.

"No," I said, finally.

"Because you think I might be right?" he asked.

"Not even close, but I will give you that this investigating stuff is a lot harder than it looks."

"So you're going to leave it to the professionals and stop getting involved?" His voice rose slightly, probably hopeful I might actually listen this time.

I shook my head. "I don't mind you and your dad thinking Fergie did it, because I *know* she didn't. And I'm going to prove it."

Alex sighed. "Okay." After a moment, he added, "But please do me a favor, Pepper." He stopped on the sidewalk a few blocks from my place.

"What's that?" I asked, coming to a stop as well.

"Give me your phone." His fingers curled twice as he made a grabbing gesture.

My hands clutched my bag defensively. "What? Why?"

"Trust me." His eyes darkened as he watched me.

I slipped my phone from the front pocket of my bag. "You gonna put some sort of tracker on it so you know where I am all the time?" I asked as I handed the thing over.

He shook his head. "No, I'm giving you my number so you can call me the next time you decide to investigate. If you're going to insist on doing this, you need someone who has some semblance of training by your side."

Pursing my lips for a second, I asked, "And why is that?"

"Because what we did back there was some sort of crash course on what *not* to do when questioning a witness." He jabbed a thumb toward the inn. After a second of silence, he handed my phone back and said, "I meant it when I said I didn't want you to get yourself killed, too. Please let me help you."

I pulled in a deep breath as he shoved his hands into his pockets. I was about to start walking again when I heard a bark I recognized.

"Hamburger?" I said, letting my word settle into the darkness around us.

Alex stared at me like my brain might be broken. "What? Are you hungry?" His thick eyebrows furrowed together.

I laughed, shook my head, and was about to explain when that bark sounded again. This time it was followed by the click-click-click of little nails on concrete. Around the corner, my dog came into view, all smiles and lolling tongue. My heart felt light and happy for the first time that night. Her happy little scrunched face was just what I needed after a depressing evening trying—and failing—to catch a murderer.

Hammy's purple leash was pulled taut and Liv rounded the corner a few steps after her, looking slightly flustered.

My grin widened. "Hamburger! Liv! Hey! What are you two doing here?"

Liv swiped a hand across her forehead, seemingly grateful for the break. "Oh, you know, letting a fifteen-pound dog yank me around, for fun. Like you do."

She looked like she was about to make another cut about Hammy's lack of leash etiquette, but her blue eyes settled on Alex. Standing up straight and shooting him her brightest, all-teeth-businesslady-let's-close-this-deal smile, Liv extended her non-leash-holding hand.

"Hello, I'm Liv—this one's roommate." She jerked her head in my direction.

"Alex." He took her hand and shook it, but then turned back to me. "I'm sorry—Pepper, did you name your dog Hamburger?"

Liv bit back a laugh, pressing her lips together.

"My niece did, technically," I said.

He nodded.

"But we call her Hammy," I said

"Or Hamdog," Liv added.

"Hamburguesa." I shrugged, adding in Fergie's Spanish version. Liv raised an eyebrow in approval.

Alex laughed. "Alright." He knelt down to pet Hammy with both hands, scratching around her neck and ears, her favorite. "Hello there, Hamburguesa."

His tongue easily curled around the Spanish word, reminding me the guy was Latin, maybe even a fluent Spanish speaker. The cute little nickname he'd called me earlier wafted back into my mind and I wondered yet again what it meant. Now, however, with Liv looking at us like she wanted to mash our faces together like Barbie and Ken dolls to make us kiss, was decidedly not the time to inquire about that.

I picked at a hangnail. "I can walk with Liv the rest of the way home. Thanks for the company."

Scratching Hammy on the top of her head one last time, he stood up and nodded.

"Anytime." After this word his gaze grabbed onto mine and he leaned closer to me, saying, "I mean that." His serious, taut face turned toward Liv and a wide smile spread across it. "Nice to meet you, Liv."

"Yeah," she breathed out the word, obviously flustered, and I was glad to see I wasn't the only one affected by his smooth smile.

As soon as he turned his back to us, holding a hand up in a goodbye, Liv latched onto my arm.

"What was that last bit all about, huh? Asking you out?" She waggled her eyebrows and shoved me twice with her elbow.

Scoffing, I shook my head and took Hammy's leash from her. "Oh, ye of great misunderstanding. What you mistook as asking me out was, in actuality, a poorly veiled attempt to threaten me into letting him tag along if I do anymore investigating."

Liv's shoulders sank and her eyelids drooped as she swooned. "Aww. Cute. He's worried about you, Peps."

"Please." I turned for home. "He only wants to follow me so he can meet his daily quota of snarky comments and feed his ever-expanding ego." Hammy trotted along next to me and I could hear Liv's footsteps close behind.

"Okay. Whatever you say." Liv caught up to me and threaded her arm through mine, falling in step. I exhaled relief as her words signaled an end to the onslaught of teasing. But a heaviness remained in my chest.

I hadn't missed the high, singsong lilt to Liv's "Okay" and I knew she thought I was fooling myself. Which was fine. Liv had a lot of opinions about what I did and I rarely listened to her, mostly because she usually suggested ridiculous things like "you should visit the gym once in a while" and "not spend all day reading"... yeah, right.

As we walked, the heaviness kept pressing down on my lungs, though, making it feel like I'd sucked in more air than I could properly utilize. Was I feeling that way because I knew she was right about Alex?

Or did I hope she was?

I wasn't sure which was worse.

14

Liv skipped and let out a little squeal of delight the next evening as we exited campus and crossed the street toward downtown. We were heading to my sister, Maggie's house for dinner and were both way too excited for a home-cooked meal we didn't have to work for—correction: Liv didn't have to work for—I would probably still get stuck with dish duty.

The air had a bite to it, but the sun was shining. Besides the odd shiver here and there, it was delightful outside. Maggie lived about a half mile from campus, so we ignored her offer to come pick us up, opting to walk instead.

I wanted to bring dessert and we swung by Bittersweet to pick something up on our way over. The doughy scents swirling from the open doors enticed me like an anthropomorphic mist, forming a hand and hooking its fingers into my nostrils to pull me closer.

Pine Crest residents always joked about being too small of a town to have a separate coffee shop *and* bakery. But behind this teasing was a deep-seated pride for our town's gem of a one-stop-shop when it came to caffeine, sugar, flour, and butter. There was even a book-sharing shelf with a great rotating selection for those times when our local bookstore, Simon's Books, happened to be closed—or you were mostly broke, like me.

As we entered, I experienced a dichotomous roller coaster of reactions. Soaring high on the just-about-heavenly smells, my stomach simultaneously twisted as my metaphorical coaster took a nosedive at the sight of Newt behind the counter. Ugh. I had forgotten how he was technically on my list of suspects for this murder until now.

"Evening, ladies," he crooned. The way he said *ladies*, all drawn out and like seventy percent *"sssssss"* made me hate the word.

My eyes landed on a sign by the register which read, "Under New Ownership." I wondered how the baker, Char, was doing with the recent change from good-natured Kathy to creepy Newt.

"Hey Nate," Liv chirped. An amused grin pulled wide across her face. She practically skipped up to the counter.

Having grown up in Seattle, where she didn't even know her neighbors and saw new people everyday, Liv was still engrossed in the novelty of small-town living. She loved how we all knew each other, and had since before we could gossip. Mostly, I think she appreciated out-of-the-ordinary people—and Pine Crest had an abundance of those. To her, Nate Newton was interesting and eccentric, far from the slithery, Naked Newt the rest of us saw in him.

"Olivia." He tipped his head in her direction, pursing his lips even more. "Pepper." His dark eyes roamed over me, leaving my skin shivery and clammy everywhere they settled. "What can I do for you this fine evening?"

Liv scrunched her shoulders up excitedly. "We're here to buy a pie. What kinds do you have?" She peeked over at me, barely suppressing a squeal of delight. Liv loved his gruesome descriptions.

"Ah... well, the cherry is particularly delicious today. Charlotte really outdid herself. The filling has a lovely sanguine color to it."

I wrinkled my nose.

"Or the apple lattice crumble," he continued. "Supple bodies of dough, delightfully dismembered, laid to rest in a pleasing pattern browned to perfection." He made an "mmmmm" face, smacking his lips together and letting his eyelids slide half closed.

I gagged a little. Liv beamed; she was having too much fun with this.

"Are you comparing my desserts to bodies again?" A twangy voice called out from the kitchen.

Newt cleared his throat.

Char, the baker behind the amazing creations lining the shelves, shoved the top half of her body through the swinging aluminum door leading to the kitchen. Her right hand held a doughy spatula, which she pointed at the tall man.

"I'm serious, I will quit as fast as you can spit if you keep up that creepy manner of speakin'." Char pursed her lips and leveled a glare at the tall man.

I guess *that* answered my question about how she felt about her new boss.

Mad as she seemed, it was still good to see Char. She'd moved to Pine Crest from Georgia when I was six. I ate up her southern accent almost as much as her famous scones. Basically, the woman ruined me for baked goods from an early age. After savoring one of her confections, I was never able to enjoy the processed, preserved, packaged imposters sitting in boxes on the grocery store shelves.

Small as she was, she had "a giant's strength," that one, spending time when she wasn't baking, running or biking every inch of Pine Crest and beyond. For an indulgent moment—because the way they were glaring at each other, it seemed like a good possibility—I mentally pictured a Battle Royale between Char and Newt. My short fantasy confirmed my suspicions that the buff baker would most definitely kick his tall, tiny, hiney.

"Charlotte, I was merely indulging the ladies in an alternate sensory experience of—"

"Nate," she snapped. "I don't want your excuses. Just cut it out, would you?" She let her gaze settle on us and a more amiable mask clicked into place over the annoyed one she'd been wearing while glaring at Newt. "Good evenin' girls! Anything I can do for you?"

"We're picking up a pie to take to Maggie's." I craned my neck as I perused the bakery display case. "I think we'll go with the cherry," I said, pointing and checking with Liv to make sure it sounded good.

Liv nodded emphatically and mouthed the word "sanguine," winking.

"Alright, well you let me know if I can help you with anythin' or if this one starts describin' food like an episode of CSI again." Char slipped back into the kitchen, muttering something about how she was gonna kill Kathy for letting "that man" buy the place.

Newt bowed a little, ignoring Char and focusing on the pie we'd picked. "Good choice," he said, giving the last word a good amount of snake hiss. He slid open the case and began packing up the pie for us.

Liv wet her lips, staring after the golden brown saucer as he slid it into a box. Once it was out of sight, and she out of its trance-like hold, she elbowed me and jerked her head toward Newt.

"Suspect. Get alibi." Her whispered words were shoved through suddenly clenched teeth.

Right. Unlikely as it was Newt had been doing anything other than creeping everyone out on campus that night, it would help to cross his name off our list. I sucked in a breath and stepped closer to the counter.

"So, Nate..." I trailed my finger along the polished cement, regretting the motion when it caught on something sticky. Rubbing my fingertips together, I peered up to where the tall man leered at me expectantly. "Um... What were you up to on campus Tuesday when I ran into you?"

His pale lip curled up into a sneer. "Simply taking care of the competition."

Liv swallowed audibly next to me. I felt my expectations catch in my throat, making it hard to breathe for a moment.

Well, that was ominous...

What competition? The part of my brain that spent more time than it should considering the validity of conspiracy theories answered back with *British accent competition?*

Blinking, I asked, "What—er—a competition?"

His dark eyes went almost black. "I wasn't about to be outdone by some out-of-towner."

Scrunching my forehead together in thought, I tried to keep my pounding heart quiet so I could form a coherent thought.

Dr. Campbell was an out-of-towner, for sure. Maybe I'd been wrong to discount this guy as a suspect. Newt did seem like someone who might know a lot about Shakespeare—the fake British accent couldn't be where the obsession stopped —and he would've given Snape a run for his Galleons for the position of Potions Prof at Hogwarts—that is to say, the man looked like he knew something about poisons.

Liv, captain of team "Newt is merely entertainingly weird instead of lock-you-in-the-basement creepy," stood there in stunned silence, lips slightly parted in defeat.

"Out—outdone?" I stuttered. My thoughts raced by like a poet on a mission against punctuation.

"That 'espresso' stand in the student center was gaining a little too much buzz around campus, if you know what I mean." He cocked a thin eyebrow.

Face flushing at the sudden letdown of adrenaline—and a little bit from nausea after he made that particular face—I exhaled my accusations in a huff.

"Campus Cup? What about them?" Liv asked, seemingly better at recovering than I. "Everyone knows their coffee sucks. No one goes there unless they're desperate."

I snorted. "Yeah, I don't think they're gaining anything but possible health code violations."

Liv said, "Nice!" as she turned to give me a high five for the burn.

Newt's pasty jaw clenched tight. "Regardless. I am under the impression Kathy was far too friendly with them and I wanted to make sure they knew there was a new general in charge."

Yeah, a frustrated fake British one, I thought to myself with a chuckle.

"You mean, you only went there to tell them—what exactly?" Liv asked.

He scoffed. "That their sad excuse for a coffee stand is a blemish on the name of the beverage and how I am going to slice them off the face of this town once and for all."

Creepy as Newt's statement was, it wasn't a confession of murder.

"This threatening you did, was it before or after you saw me?" I asked.

Newt pushed back his shoulders. "Before our conversation."

Welp. There was his alibi then. By the time I found Dr. C, his body was starting to grow cold, which meant he had to have been deceased for at least a half an hour.

"I still don't see why you're worried about that crappy stand." I scanned the cute, clean, heavenly smelling café. "There are a few thousand students on campus, not to mention the almost two thousand full-time Pine Crest residents. I'd say there's enough business for the both of you. Heck, we could probably even use another shop or two the way the line wraps around this building in the mornings."

Kathy, the previous owner, often complained about the rigorous pace, saying she wished for the quiet, steady flow which settled over the café each summer. I hadn't been able to talk with her since she'd sold the place to Newt, but I was guessing she'd finally made the decision to do something less stressful with her time.

"Regardless," Newt answered, tightly. I saw a flicker of... something in those dark eyes. "It's run by some whiny scamp from the city who only shows up once a quarter to make sure the rickety thing isn't on fire. He doesn't even train his baristas... if you can even call his employees that."

"Who'd you talk to at Campus Cup?" Liv asked Newt, working her bottom lip in between her teeth. I recognized her embarrassed tic and my interest piqued.

"Some floppy-haired part-time employee." Newt rolled his eyes, saying the word "employee" as if it were a disease.

"Was it Carson?" Liv asked, cheeks turning pink.

"Tell me, Olivia, do you remember the name of every insignificant bug you crush upon finding it in your apartment?" Newt's lips pursed smugly when he saw both Liv and I were speechless. "That's what I thought." He turned to continue boxing up our pie.

Liv's eyes were wide when they met mine. "Wait, the bugs have names?" she whispered. Our stunned faces broke into smiles as we suppressed giggles. After paying, we toted our delicious spoils toward the door.

"Pepper," Newt's voice stopped me as my fingers curled over the handle.

I turned around. Newt narrowed his eyes in a way which made my knees wobble unsteadily for a moment as if I were a lanky piece of prey and he knew I wouldn't be able to outrun him.

"Give my regards to Margaret."

"Will do," I said.

Escaping out into the fresh air, we fast-walked toward Maggie's house until we were well out of view of the shop. Only then did we stop to catch our breath, rolling wild eyes at each other as we recovered from *all of that.*

"Well, that was terrifying." I let a shiver remove the worst of the goosebumps that had formed on my skin.

"I kind of agree with you for once." Liv ran her hands up and down her arms. "All of that squashing bugs and slicing blemishes. Eww."

"Yeah, so much of it was disturbing, not the least of which was how he knew we live in an apartment."

Liv cringed. "Lucky guess?"

"We can only hope."

Somewhat recovered, we started walking again. A question tugged at my mind.

"Hey, why'd you ask him about who was working at Campus Cup when he went on his pimple-themed threat rampage?"

I glanced at Liv out of the corner of my eye and noticed her shoulders stiffen. Something was up and I wanted to get to the bottom of it. My sleuthing didn't have to be limited to murder investigations, after all.

She shrugged. "Oh, you know, so we could make sure his alibi checks out. It's not enough to believe whatever people say they were doing, Pepper. A real detective double-checks. People lie." At this last statement, she met my gaze finally.

"Yeah, people like you." I scoffed. "Since when are you interested in Carson Moore?" I pulled up a mental picture of the laid back, class-clown head of campus activities.

Liv cleared her throat. "I—there isn't—I've had a stressful couple of weeks with my classes and stopped by the stand to grab coffee a few times when I couldn't make it out here and back. No big deal. I met him a few times. We talked."

I stopped. She'd been giving me too hard a time about Alex for me to let this drop.

"Since when do you blush when talking about someone you've met a few times?" I asked, sidling up to a garbage can on the street and holding the pie over the opening.

Liv's eyes widened and she took a step forward, hands outstretched. "Now, now. There's no need to involve the pie; it's innocent."

I cocked an eyebrow. "Just tell me the truth and it'll be safe."

Sighing, Liv let her shoulders drop. "Okay. I like him. He's fun, makes me laugh."

I pulled the pie back from the trashy precipice and tucked it under my arm. "See? That wasn't so hard."

We started walking toward Maggie's again, but after a few silent steps—where I may or may not have been smiling victoriously—Liv said, "You better watch the cocky act, Brooks, or I might have to tattle to Alex and let him know you're investigating without him."

Now it was her turn to curl her lips in triumph as she walked ahead of me, stopping at Maggie's house.

Right. I gulped and followed her through the gate.

15

"Hey," Maggie called from the kitchen as we walked inside her house.

Garlic and butter permeated the warm air inside. We took off our coats and hung them by the door.

"Mags, it smells amazing in here," I said, closing my eyes for a moment. I could hear Liv take sips of the air next to me, too.

We rounded the corner, into the large kitchen, where Maggie and Josh were positioned around the island in various stages of chopping and sautéing.

Maggie smiled big and bright, her brown hair piled loosely into a bun on the top of her head. After setting down the pie on the counter, I wrapped my arms around her, almost unable to reach with her pregnant belly in between us, and then leaned down to plant a quick kiss on my soon-to-be nephew. Maggie didn't love it when people around town came up and touched her belly, but I was different—I was family.

"Hey Hudson," I told her belly. I still wanted to giggle

every time I thought of him possibly being named Hamburger. "You coming out anytime soon, man?"

Maggie sighed and Josh laughed from where he stood cutting up an onion, saying, "Two weeks to go."

"Ooh, pie?" Maggie wiped her hands on a towel and made a beeline for the pie on the counter.

"Yeah, Newt says hello." I winked, waiting for the reaction I knew was coming.

Maggie shivered and stepped away from the dessert.

"Don't worry, Char made it. Newt only boxed it up for us," Liv said, plopping herself onto one of the bar stools around the kitchen island.

"And royally creeped us out while he did so," I added.

Maggie rolled her eyes. "What's new?"

Liv grabbed an olive from the jar on the counter. "Well, he's definitely not a murderer," she said as she chewed. "That's new."

Tipping her head, my sister returned to the items on her stovetop. "That we can *prove*," she mumbled, moving the veggies around in the pan.

"Actually, Margaret, this time he's the least of our worries." I raised my eyebrows and smirked, knowing she hated her full name and how Newt had insisted on calling her by it since elementary school.

I was growing increasingly sure Newt had some sort of love-like obsession with my sister, but I wasn't going to knowingly incur the wrath of a pregnant woman by mentioning my theory.

Most likely too tired to deal with my teasing, Maggie ignored the name and focused on my statement. "You're still going on about this murder investigation?"

Liv scoffed. "And on and on." She met a grin from Josh with one of her own.

I sat next to Liv. "Because I know it's Evilsworth. It has to be."

Josh sliced through a bunch of spinach and then froze. He set the knife down and furrowed his brow. "What makes you so sure?"

I started my list, flicking a finger up each time I added something new. "Dr. C had attacked his new book—which he loves so much he can't go five minutes without talking about it. He hates Fergie, which would explain him threatening her with the second note. He got in a huge fight with the victim a mere half hour before he was killed. And…" I pulled in a breath as I thought. "He's just terrible." I let my hand drop and settle on the cool countertop.

"What about a weapon?" Maggie asked. "Did they ever figure out what killed the poor guy?"

"Poison," I said, watching my sister transfer the veggies from the pan onto a serving dish already full of steaming pasta. "Hebanon."

Maggie scrunched up her nose. "What's that?"

"Most likely made up by Shakespeare, but it could be Hensbane, Western Hemlock, or a myriad of other poisons prevalent during The Bard's time."

Josh coughed in that surprised way people do when they suck in air too quickly. The three of us glanced over at him. Slightly red-faced, he waved a hand and shook his head, motioning he was fine.

"And you think Evilsworth has access to that kind of stuff?" Maggie asked, turning back to me.

Leave it to my sister to find the one flaw in my theory.

"Um… well, I haven't found any proof he *doesn't*."

Maggie put a hand on her hip. "And someone's threatening Fergie now?"

I wobbled my head back and forth. "Possibly."

My sister sighed. "Peps, I don't like you getting involved with this. It sounds dangerous."

"Alex keeps telling her the same thing, but she won't listen to him either." Liv's betrayal rang loudly off the high ceilings in my sister's perfect eggshell-colored kitchen.

I shot a "thanks a lot" look in her direction. She mouthed "sorry" as I turned to face what I knew was about to turn into *a thing*. Maggie's lips were pursed together and her brown eyes sparkled as if someone told her she could spend as much money as she wanted at Ann Taylor Loft.

"And *who* is Alex?" she asked.

Liv, who probably figured she was already in deep enough trouble and she might as well have fun with it, helped with that clarification. "Oh, he's the hot guy from the library whose dad is in charge of the investigation and who Pepper wants to lick."

At that, Josh chuckled. I narrowed my eyes at him. He went back to chopping. Maggie, however, could've been in the running for some Guinness Book world record for "smallest forehead" with how close her eyebrows were to her hairline.

I shook my head. "That's not true. Well—the last part isn't, at least." I grumbled. "The man is infuriating. Not lickable in the least. I'm only letting him tag along because he sometimes slips up and gives me information about the case. He wants me to stay out of it because he thinks Fergie did it."

Liv chimed in, finishing a sentence I had *thought* was complete. "But he knows she's still going to investigate and wants to be there so he can keep her safe. Isn't that sweet?"

Maggie nodded. "I like the sound of this guy."

"Big surprise," I said, rolling my eyes.

If I needed another rationale to keep my distance from

Alex, I wasn't going to get a better reason than Maggie's approval.

Maggie clapped her hands together. "Okay, we're pretty much ready to eat. Will you go get Brooklyn? She's playing up in her room."

Happy for any excuse to leave this lions den disguised as a kitchen, I was out of there before Maggie even finished her directive. Brooklyn may have only been three, but she was a fierce supporter of her Aunty Pepper and I really needed an ally if I was going to make it through dinner.

LIKE THE CHAMP fighter she was, Brooklyn distracted the table with songs from her favorite movies and stories about her invisible friend, Larry. The kid was good and I was glad to have her in my corner.

"Daddy, why do you look like you swallowed a bug?" Brooklyn asked close to half an hour into our dinner. Her nose bunched up as she put her fork down. "Do you not like spinach either?" She held her hand up to her mouth—placing it on the wrong side and therefore directing her words right at my sister. "If you plug your nose, you can't taste it too much."

My shoulders shook through a stifled laugh. I could see Liv's mouth twist in an effort to do the same. Maggie sighed.

While the rest of the table was absorbed in my niece's adorable comment, my eyes slipped over to my brother-in-law. Brooklyn had a point. Josh appeared sweaty, and a pale grimace had settled over his normally tanned, handsome features. My mind flashed back to his odd behavior earlier when I'd mentioned the murder investigation. Either he really did eat something that wasn't agreeing with him, or Josh had more information about this case.

After Liv's earlier betrayal, I didn't feel the least bit bad about what I did next.

"Maggie, after hearing your thoughts on Alex, I can't wait to get your take on the new guy Liv is head-over-heels about." I turned my head slowly to meet Liv's wide, stabby gaze. "Liv, why don't you tell her all about Carson?" Pulling my lips into a Cheshire Cat grin, I watched my sister take the bait.

Once Liv was squirming under Maggie's interrogation, I turned to Josh.

"Wanna help me clear the table?"

He nodded warily. I could feel my sister's eyes watch us in her peripheral vision, but if she suspected anything of her husband's odd behavior, the chance to grill Liv about Carson proved too sweet a treat to pass up.

Josh and I collected as many dishes as we could, and then headed into the kitchen. After squirting probably too much soap into the sink, I blocked the drain and started the water, then spun to confront the distracted man behind me.

"Okay. What gives, man?" I whispered as forcefully as I could without the others hearing.

Josh's chest heaved. He set the dishes on the counter and then ran a hand through his hair. "Pepper, I think I made a huge mistake."

Blood hammering in my ears, I tried to focus. "What?"

"Remember when I said I knew it wasn't Danny?"

"Yeah."

He shook his head. "I'm starting to doubt that."

"Why? What happened?"

Josh turned, paced away from me, and then swiveled back around. "I already told the police it couldn't have been him, but—" He paused, his eyes sliding to the dining room and then back to me. "Danny's been sharing a lot more lately, about his daughter especially. He's fighting for shared custody, something finally within his grasp now that he has a steady job and a clean slate with the law for the last few months." Josh's blue eyes darkened. "He got worked up the other day and was ranting about how if he lost this job, he would surely lose his case." Josh leaned closer, swallowing once more before whispering, "He said he'd make sure whomever was to blame live to regret it."

Lips parted as I took in the new information, I exhaled in understanding. "And Dr. Campbell threatened to get him fired." Seeing the sink was almost full, I shut off the water and then looked back to Josh.

He nodded and his brows were furrowed so tightly they were nearly a unibrow. "Then when you brought up the poison tonight…"

Spine straightening, I craned my neck closer as Josh's voice dropped now that we no longer had the rushing water to cover up our conversation.

"Danny's mom is a local homeopath, or something." He shook his head. "She's helping him a lot with the trial, with getting back custody of Lila. And in return, he's going out and gathering a lot of the plants she uses for her medications."

Eyes rolling to the ceiling, I tried to think of how that implicated the man. Luckily, Josh went on.

"We went out to lunch yesterday and he drove. He's got a bunch of bags sitting in his car." Josh's stare held mine. "Pepper, he told me not to touch any of them because there was some poisonous stuff."

I pulled in a deep breath, nose bunching. "Why would she use poisonous plants?"

Josh's face let go of some of its tension. "I asked the same thing. Apparently homeopaths believe 'like cures like.' If you want to cure pain, you've got to give it something that causes pain. He said it's used only in small doses, tiny in fact, but he gets large amounts at one time so she can dry it out and save it up."

"Large enough to…" I curled my toes in my socks.

Josh nodded.

I pulled in a deep breath. "But if he was guilty, why would he go around telling you all of this?"

"I don't know. Maybe he was dying to confess to someone. Villains do it all the time in movies. That could be based on real life."

"True." I tapped my fingers on the counter. "But I really don't think Danny did this. Evilsworth is the murderer. I just know it. No one has a better motive than him. Don't worry."

"You two aren't eating that whole pie by yourselves in there, are you?" Maggie's voice sang into the kitchen.

We glanced at each other. Josh dipped his head toward the pie. "You take it in. I'll get these dishes rinsed and loaded."

The amount of pie I've eaten in my life must've been exponentially more than I can recall, or maybe I was a waitress at some roadside diner in another life, because my body seemed to instinctually know the routine. I managed to cut and serve the table dessert even though my mind was still focused on what Josh had divulged. Despite my suggestion to Josh not to worry, I couldn't seem to make myself do the same.

It's a testament to Char's bakery magic that once I sat down to eat my own slice, the soft, flaky crust and sweet-but-at-the-same-time-tart cherry filling stole my attention away from Josh's suspicions about Danny. Each new, delicious bite calmed me. So much so, by the time Liv and I were making our way to the door a while later, I was almost positive we didn't have anything to worry about.

Josh pulled me off to the side as Liv and Maggie said their goodbyes. "You be careful with all of this, Pepper." He pulled me into a hug.

"I will." I turned my attention to my sister, squeezing her and sinking into her familiar arms for a second. "Thanks, Mags. Call if you need anything. I can come watch Brooklyn whenever this guy decides to come out and meet us." I patted her belly goodbye.

Maggie cupped my face in her hands and then leaned in close to kiss me on the cheek. "Thanks. Love you."

I shrugged on my jacket and sidled up to Liv who stood with her hand on the doorknob.

"Teasing about Alex aside," Maggie said, pinning me in place with a serious glare, "I think you should listen to the guy. I would feel better if you had someone around watching your back." She wore the same pleading expression she used when we were growing up and she didn't want me to tell Mom and Dad a secret.

Threading my arm through Liv's, I winked. "Don't worry. I've got this girl by my side. We're good. I promise. Night, Brooklyn," I called into the other room even though I'd already gotten my goodnight squeeze from the little munchkin.

Liv and I stepped out into the cold before my sister could make any more ominous statements. We kept our arms intertwined as we walked home. While campus felt like a somewhat worrisome place right now with a killer on the loose and all, being in town still felt like my safe space. The colorful buildings and houses crowded around us like a protective hug.

After a block or so, Liv cleared her throat. "Sorry about giving up the Alex intel…" In the glow from the streetlights, I could see my best friend frown.

"It's okay. Sorry about telling her about Carson. It really wasn't as much retribution as a needed distraction."

"For what?"

I recounted what Josh had told me about Danny and his fears the man wasn't innocent.

Liv blew out an exhale. "Whoa. That's pretty big. Don't you think?"

Shaking my head, I said, "Not really. Evilsworth's our guy, Liv."

"Okay… if you're sure."

"I am." We rounded the street and our apartment complex came into view. "See? I don't need Alex around to babysit me. I was able to find out information about the case and shockingly lived to tell about it."

I let go of Liv's arm and winked at her as I dug in my pocket for my keys. But as we stepped closer to our apartment, I realized, with a sinking feeling, I didn't need them.

The door was already open.

It wasn't wide open, but had been pushed far enough that it wasn't latched. In the sliver of space between the door and the jam, sat a notecard.

Trembling fingers reaching, I plucked the thick paper and the door snicked the rest of the way open, swinging slow and wide. The gray exterior of the apartment complex swirled around me as my eyes lit on the handwriting I'd seen twice already.

Come not within the measure of my wrath.

My eyes rolled in fear as I finally registered the now-open entrance to our home.

"Hammy." The word left my mouth in a heavy whisper then sank like a stone. I dropped the card and ran inside.

Her body was limp, spilling out of her little teal dog bed. My stomach clenched together in fear.

"Oh no. Hammy, I—" I knelt down next to her, my hands shaking again as I reached forward, not wanting to feel the coldness I knew in my gut my fingertips would meet. Tears welled in my eyes, but I couldn't bring myself to wipe them away.

A snort made me jump. Hammy's body writhed and her legs windmilled in the air for a moment as she grunted into a standing position, eyes wide. When her gaze landed on me, her pink tongue lolled out of her mouth and she pranced forward into my already outstretched arms.

"Sweet baby Jesus, thank you," Liv whispered behind me. "She seem okay?"

I met my roommate's eyes, almost electric in their intensity and then nodded. "I think so." My hands swiped all over Hammy's furry body. The dog leaned into me, snorting some more in her enjoyment, unaware this was not merely another petting session. "I think she really was just sound asleep."

Shaking my head, I stood, pulling Hammy into my arms with me. I wasn't letting that dog out of my sight for a good while, if I could help it.

"I think you're going to have to eat your words, Pepper." Liv shook her head, running her hands up and down what were probably goose-bump-covered arms. "Because now seems like a really good time to call Alex."

Swallowing, I nodded. "Actually, now seems like a good time to call his father."

16

After the police arrived, questioned us—as well as some of our neighbors—and convinced our apartment management to add a dead bolt to our door, there were only a few hours left for sleep.

Ha. Not that we could relax *at all* after the break-in.

We curled together on the couch. Hammy was squeezed between us and we wrapped ourselves tight in all the blankets we could find. And then we stared at the door, at the new dead bolt.

That's not to say we got *no* sleep. I woke with a start at six and Liv's head was resting on my shoulder as the blankets moved up and down with her slumbering breath. She blinked awake soon after and we decided to get up. Even though we had a pretty good excuse to skip our classes today, we wanted the distraction.

Whatever sleep we had gotten, however, was obviously far from enough. Exhaustion weighed on my body as we walked Hammy to Maggie's to stay for the day and a massive yawn pulled at the corners of my mouth as we stumbled into Bittersweet on our way back toward campus.

Newt must've heard what happened already, because when Liv and I walked in, he proffered two of the largest to-go cups I'd ever seen toward us. Not only did we get to skip the line, but he wouldn't let us pay a cent.

Grateful smiles pulled at our tired faces, but after about two minutes into our walk toward campus, neither of us had taken the first sip. I kept shooting mine pensive looks and holding it close to check if I could smell anything weird—'cause, you know, I totally know what poison smells like.

"He did seem to know where we live..." Liv said, her words stepping out on shaky limbs as she narrowed her eyes at her own drink.

Wetting my lips, I nodded. "We *had* questioned him only hours before the break-in. And he had these coffees ready for us..."

"He had an alibi, though."

My fingers closed even tighter around the coffee. "Detour to see the new boyfriend to confirm it?" I tilted my head in question.

Liv must've been too tired to roll her eyes at me, because she simply nodded and we picked up our pace toward the student center.

Still-full coffees sloshed in our hands as we approached the cart that made up the sad-excuse-for-a-latte stand that was the Campus Cup. There wasn't a line wrapped around the block, like at Bittersweet, but there was more of a gathering than I had expected. A gathering of girls, to be exact. Five ladies I knew to be founding members of the "Bring the Greek System Back to NWU" coalition, stood in various states of posing.

There was so much pouting, chest flaunting, leg lengthening, and hair flipping that I actually looked around for cameras—an impromptu fashion shoot in a small state college might be a thing, right?

It turned out that, nope, it wasn't. These sultry students were focused on—none other than—Liv's new guy.

Carson stood behind the cart, pulling levers, pouring liquids, and pumping syrups. He was cute. That had never been up for debate. With his easy smile, brown swoopy hair, and his deep blue eyes, the guy was almost as swoon-worthy as I, annoyingly, found Alex. No, it was his goofy, frat-boy-esque personality that made me question Liv's interest.

As we stood there, Carson barked out a low whoop, followed by, "Steve-O! Drink's up, buddy." Then he slid the full cup along the cart's countertop.

Liv watched him, enraptured. I inwardly shook my head. Love truly knew no bounds.

As we watched, the person I can only assume was Steve-O, lunged forward and grabbed the cup right as it rocketed off the edge. The coffee spent a good second in the air before he caught it. The onlookers gasped and clapped as Steve-O stood up with the intact order, raising his hands above his head as if he'd performed a difficult dismount off the pommel horse at the Olympics.

"Maybe Newt wasn't being paranoid," I mumbled. "This place does look a lot busier than normal."

Before Liv could answer me, Carson's deep blue eyes locked on us. "As I *Liv* and breathe! What a surprise." He wiped his hands on a cloth and stepped out from behind the cart.

While I approved of the way his face broke into a full grin at the sight of my best friend—darn right she deserved someone who lit up when he saw her—I wasn't crazy about the daggers being thrown at us from the heavily mascaraed eyes of Carson's group of admirers.

Just then, something else caught my eye. Behind the student center, through the floor-to-ceiling windows, I saw one of the university's utility vans. Danny opened the sliding side door and kneeled just inside, fiddling with some electronic equipment.

Liv smiled and stepped forward, splitting my attention. "Hey Carson."

He gave her chin an adorable little tug with his thumb and pointer finger and then tipped his head toward me, saying, "Hey, Peps. How goes it?"

I smiled a hello to him and then shot Liv an incredulous look as she glanced back toward me. Given how my best friend basically had hearts for eyes as she looked at Carson, I decided to humor her even though she didn't deserve it with the way she'd acted around Alex the other day.

Or maybe... I could use this opportunity to go question Danny. After the break-in, I was more motivated than ever to get this whole thing behind me.

I took two steps, but Carson placed both of his hands on his chest and leaned back a little.

"You *trying* to stab me straight in the heart?" he asked

I thought he was talking about me leaving, so I stopped. But then I noticed he was focused on our coffees, stamped with the Bittersweet logo.

Pink color rushed to Liv's cheeks and she shoved her drink into my free hand, causing me to divert all of my attention to these two love birds instead of watching Danny outside. I was about to scoff and ask what in the name of Espresso was wrong with her—I *know* the woman did *not* just choose a guy over good coffee—when she stepped toward Carson and put a delicate hand on his apron-covered chest. His eyebrows shot up and the charming grin on his face turned sly.

"Carson, Pepper and I don't have much time, but I needed to ask you a question."

His lip curved up on one side. "Anything."

"Did that guy from Bittersweet come talk to you the other evening? It would've been Tuesday?" Liv checked with me and then turned back toward Carson when I nodded.

Carson's brow furrowed. "Yeah, he did. It was super weird. He said some creepy stuff about zits, I think, and then he was gone." Carson rubbed the back of his neck and added, "It was right when I was trying to close, like six thirty."

"So he was only there for a moment?" she asked.

Carson shook his head, freeing a few locks of hair from the gelled swoop. "I wish. The guy sat there staring at me for almost an hour before he approached and threaten me." Carson pointed to one of the tables nearby. "He watched me like he was thinking of how best to cook me up and eat me." Carson shivered.

The evidence clicked into place in both Liv's and my brain at the same time, it seemed, because our eyes locked.

Newt's alibi checked out. He was *not* the murderer. Which meant…

I frantically tipped my coffee back at the same time I shoved Liv's forward into her waiting hands. She took a long sip from hers, letting her eyelids flutter in the ecstasy of the moment.

Carson stood there with that grin still curling up his lips. Liv turned back toward him.

"Thanks, Moore. See you later." She held up her coffee. "We gotta run."

Right. Class. I glanced outside quickly. Maybe I could still catch—nope, the white van was gone. Crap. I'd missed Danny a second time. Turning in the opposite direction, I caught up with my friend as she reached the doors out to the square, an outdoor seating area next to the student center. Our classes were in separate directions, but before we split up, she raised her coffee to me. "Proost."

I raised mine back. "Salud."

We liked to add culture to our drinking—both alcoholic and non—and were always trying out new forms of "cheers." I hoped Liv wouldn't read too much into my use of the Spanish term. I had spent a few hours on a translation site the other night trying to figure out what Alex had called me in front of Katie.

Unfortunately, I couldn't remember exactly what word he'd used and my guesses hadn't gotten me too far. Either there was something endearing I wasn't seeing in calling someone a "picnic" or I was going to have to ask the guy for clarification.

After watching Liv walk away, I turned toward the English building and sucked down my coffee, finishing it before I even stepped foot in my first class. As much as the caffeine helped, my brain was defiant and couldn't seem to focus on Professor Simms, hard as I tried to pay attention.

Ten minutes into class, my eyelids felt like they'd gained the dreaded Freshman Fifteen—each. But if I thought trying to keep my heavy lids peeled was a sign I was tired, it was nothing compared to when my eyes wandered by the door and started seeing visions of Alex standing outside my classroom.

Oh great, now I was having some sort of waking dream. Dream Alex raised his eyebrows over soft, concerned eyes, as if he was asking if I was okay.

This was officially weird. I *had* recently downed a coffee the size of most movie theater popcorn buckets, so I could very well be seeing things. But Dream Alex seemed incredibly vivid. The gears in my fatigued brain eventually picked up speed, especially when he started to motion for me to join him out in the hall. I blinked, still not completely sure if—

"Ms. Brooks, it appears you have a visitor," Professor Simms said, her voice cutting coolly across the room. "Would you mind meeting him in the hallway so my class may proceed?"

Okay, so I wasn't seeing things after all.

Cringing, I slipped from my seat and tiptoed out of class, pulling the door shut behind me as I joined Alex in the hallway.

"What are you doing here?" I asked.

Alex craned his neck forward. "What took you so long? Why were you just sitting there staring at me? I felt like an idiot standing here flailing outside of your class."

I studied the ceiling. "I—sorta—well, I didn't get much sleep last night and I thought for a minute I was imagining you standing out here."

His annoyed expression morphed into that one-sided grin. "You dream of me often, then?"

"Definitely not!" I walked a little ways down the hall and then turned back to him. "I'm tired and my brain couldn't think of a reason you'd be here, so I thought I was *hallucinating*." I accentuated the negative word.

Alex placed a hand over his chest as if my words had buried themselves there. "Ouch, Brooks. I was actually coming to see if you were all right." His joking smile dropped as he tried to meet my gaze. "I didn't see my dad until this morning. He told me there'd been a break-in at your place."

"You mean, he knows we know each other? You told him you're helping me?"

Snorting, Alex said, "Oh, absolutely not. He'd kill me if he knew about that. No, he mentioned it was the apartment of the student who'd found the body, so I came to find you."

"Oh." I pressed my lips together.

"Are you? Okay?" Those eyes of his were like dark chocolate. Delicious. Mostly bitter, but just the right amount of sweet.

I nodded.

"What about your roommate and that dog of yours, Ham Sandwich?" he asked, a sly smile pulling across his lips, showing me he was teasing.

"Hamburger." I laughed. "Yes, she and Liv are fine."

I wondered for a moment whether or not I should fill him in on all of the stuff Josh had told me about Danny. But then the knowledge that I held information I had yet to divulge to him, made me wonder if Alex might be keeping anything from me. I mean, his dad was the lead detective, after all. Maybe I could barter my intel for something he knew.

"I should probably get back," I said. "But I have some new stuff to share with you. Any chance you want to get together and..." I motioned back and for between us.

Alex raised his eyebrows. *Uh oh. Between that look and me saying—oh no...*

"Get together?" he asked.

Having been shaking my head preemptively, ever since I'd seen the look cross his face, I continued.

"Not like *that*. Just—you know—sharing stats, looking at each other's playbook."

Dear lord, what was I saying? Alex didn't seem like much of a sports guy and I knew *nothing* about any of it—as was now blatantly obvious. Hearing my words aloud, I realized my sports metaphors had made things sound even worse. *Gah! I couldn't win.*

Maybe if I employed a good ole just-friends-type of gesture...

"What do you say?" I asked, then slow-motion punched him in the arm, like pals.

Inwardly, I groaned. *I'm dying. Dead. Just going to crawl into a hole and never come out.*

Alex appeared as confused as I felt. But after a moment, the creases in his brow smoothed out and he said, "How about tonight?"

"Sure..." The word stretched out past what was comfortable, but I couldn't help it. *Tonight? Like where? At the library or for dinner?* The distinction between the two was huge. Like James Joyce's *Ulysses* huge.

When I finally stopped overanalyzing his words, I remembered going out wasn't even an option. I couldn't leave Liv alone, not after last night.

"Actually, could you come to my place?"

The suggestive look on Alex's face made me want to turn that friendly, fake punch into a real one.

"Oh, get over yourself." I scoffed. "I don't want to leave Liv and Hammy alone after... you know."

At the mention of the break-in, Alex sobered and cut the flirty act, nodding in lieu of anymore teasing. "Sounds good. I can be there by seven."

"Okay."

Alex turned to leave, calling over his shoulder. "Text me your address so I don't have to track you down this time, Brooks."

It took me a few seconds before I could wipe the smile off my face enough to go back into class.

17

I whirled around our apartment that evening like I was Mary Poppins and I'd downed about seven spoonfuls of sugar.

And, *okay*. I had to admit, that "practically perfect" nanny was kinda right; there was an element of fun in every job to be done, especially with Hammy jumping about my feet and trying to play with me the whole time I cleaned. I couldn't help but laugh at her antics.

When I finally sat down to do some homework on our spotless couch in our spotless living room, I was starting to see Liv's point about cleaning more. It felt good. But the satisfied feelings only lasted for a while, because as I sat there, the place felt so much emptier without all of our clutter everywhere. And the emptiness turned into loneliness. Which turned into fear as I remembered the notecard stuck in the open door last night.

Come not within the measure of my wrath.

It'd been a while since I'd read *The Two Gentlemen of Verona*, but from what I could recall, the play had mostly been about men fighting over women. In fact, I think that's what Valentino had been warning against when he'd spouted the line about his wrath. Common translation: *Stay away from my lady, dude. Or else.*

Which was a bit of a head scratcher. I wasn't anywhere close to being a part of a love triangle—or even a line segment, for that matter. Still, the realization that the quote had probably been taken out of context didn't diminish the creepiness or threatening nature of the line. I was getting close to the killer and they were getting scared, making mistakes again.

Yet another sliver of evidence to support my theory that Fergie hadn't done this terrible deed. The woman hated when people misused the written word—don't even get her started on people incorrectly attributing quotes. And if you saw a context-less quote as a fault, which I did, it was also the second mistake the killer had made when quoting Shakespeare.

Dr. Campbell's murderer was either someone who knew little about Shakespeare or—as I was increasingly fearing was the case—the jerk was intentionally misusing The Bard's words.

Suddenly, the doorknob jiggled and, for a moment, my heart clenched tight in my chest. I realized, all-too-late, I hadn't remembered to lock the deadbolt, still not used to the newly installed safeguard.

Had the murderer come back?

It was probably only Liv, but… there was a lot of extra fiddling happening—as if someone were picking the lock instead of inserting a key. Frozen, I couldn't seem to make my voice work to call out to whomever was on the other side of that door—not that I really expected anyone to answer to "Hey… Murderer. Is that you?"

As the lock clicked open, Hamburger leaped off the

couch like Ariel the fairy in *The Tempest*, ready to save her potent master, Prospero—or Peppero—from the evil and murderous plans of Caliban the monster. Cute as my fairy protector was with her wagging nubbin of a tail and defensive snorts, I doubted she would be able to do much against this real-life Caliban.

Finally, the door swung toward me. I clutched my notebook in front of my face. Peeking out from behind it… I swallowed my heart back down my throat as Liv strode in and shoved the door shut with her heel. Her eyes landed on me, forehead wrinkling in concern.

"Just me." She breathed the words softly, dropping her bag in our usual place by the door. "Sorry for all of the noise, I had the wrong key."

Looked like I wasn't the only one getting used to the extra lock. Exhaling my fears. I hopped up from the couch and clicked the deadbolt into place. Liv knelt next to Hamburger and scratched her back, inciting a round of satisfied puppy grunts.

Blinking, Liv glanced around the apartment. "Whoa. Did I miss something last night or did the murderer tidy up while he or she was here?"

I crossed my arms over my chest. "*I* cleaned."

She leaned back. "You what?"

"Cleaned. And if you ever want it to happen again, you'll shut down this whole act." I gestured toward her posture.

She lifted her hands in defense. "Okay, okay." Liv surveyed as she walked through the living room, nodding and pressing her lips forward. She stopped, squinted, and then disappeared into the bathroom.

When she reappeared, her head was tilted and her eyes sparkled, almost as much as I knew the tile in the shower did right now. My stomach clenched at her smug, about-to-give-me-a-hard-time expression.

"Ooooooh! Pepper's having a guy over," she trilled.

"What? No—I—this isn't..." I shook my head, fervently, giving myself instant vertigo.

"Peps, the only time I've ever seen you clean in three years was when Michael was coming over. And by the sheer impeccability of this particular cleaning job..." Liv craned her neck, double-checking the apartment and then folding her arms over her chest. "I'd say Alex is coming over."

My tongue darted out to wet my suddenly dry lips. But it did little to help them formulate an answer that wasn't going to land me in a world of elbow bumps and jeers. I wanted to lie and shake my head—if only for the momentary relief it would bring me—but I knew in less than an hour, Alex would be showing up at our door, calling my bluff.

"I can neither confirm nor deny—"

Liv pointed at me. "Oh my god, he is! He is?" Her mouth dropped open.

Head hanging slightly, I nodded. "Yes." After I let the word slip out, my hands shot up like two stop signs that might temper her reaction. "We're talking about the case. And he's only coming here because I didn't want to leave you and Hammy alone." A threatening stare helped my point hit home.

"Sure. Totally innocent. Got it." She turned away from me, probably so I couldn't see the grin spreading across her face.

"We're not even friends."

"Hmm..." Liv said, looking over her shoulder. "The lady doth protest too much, methinks."

My face broke into a huge grin and I lunged at Liv,

wrapping her into a hug-crush. "Quoting Shakespeare? You're officially my favorite. I forgive you."

Liv squirmed. "Okay, okay. Don't get too excited. I have no idea who said it or what play it's even from."

My face was deadpan. "Queen Gertrude, during the play within a play scene during *The Tragedy of Hamlet: Prince of Denmark*, and she says it in response to the play within a play which—"

"Nope," Liv interrupted me and put her hands up like stop signs. "Business major, here. No literary analysis for me. Maybe you can talk literature with Alex, though."

Pointing at her back, I said, "Don't embarrass me, Benson."

Let's just say, the wink she gave me before disappearing into her room, didn't inspire confidence.

THE RAPPING of knuckles on our door made me jump, even though the clock had warned me we were nearing seven.

After the hard time Liv had given me, I'd mussed some of the pillows on the couch, thrown a sweater here and put a dirty glass there to make it look like I hadn't spent so much time cleaning on his behalf. So when I opened the door, I felt pretty confident Alex would be neither grossed out nor suspicious of the state of our humble apartment.

Said confidence leaked out from my pores as my eyes combed up and down his tall frame. Even in his casual jeans and sweatshirt, he had a way of making me feel under-dressed—granted, I *was* wearing leggings and a second-hand sweater, but we were in my home for Pete's sake.

"Evening," he said, smiling.

"Er... come in." I stepped back to let him in as

Hamburger ran out from where she'd been snoozing in Liv's bedroom, letting out a few high-pitched barks as she pranced around my feet.

"Hey there, Hot Dog." Alex walked inside and closed the door behind him.

I shot a glare right between his eyes.

Alex put his hands up. "Sorry… Hamburger." He dipped his chin in an apology, but his face wrinkled and he added, "You realize that's not much better, right?"

The man had a point. I shrugged.

Hammy didn't seem to mind his teasing, however, because in addition to his formal apology, Alex knelt down and scratched behind her ears. After a few seconds, my fierce protector was tongue-lolling putty in his hands, looking up into his eyes lovingly.

I scrunched my toes up in my woolly socks. "Wanna tour?"

He stood and nodded. "Absolutely."

Flourishing my hand to my right, I said, "This is the sitting parlor." I used the haughty British accent Liv and I used while watching Downton Abbey. Unsure where that had come from, I decided to go with it. "We barely use the room, but our maid Flora insists we take our tea here in the evenings." I waved a hand at the worn, lumpy gray sofa Liv's dad had given us.

Alex's mouth quirked up at one end. He seemed to appreciate my weird sense of humor.

"Very nice," he said after a second.

Walking forward and doing a pirouette on the linoleum, I motioned around me at the kitchen. "And then there's the larder, of course. We spared no expense. Highest quality etcetera, etcetera." I gestured to the old oven, on which only two of the four burners worked.

Alex pressed his lips together and lifted his eyebrows.

Wafting past him, I glided to Liv's open doorway. "Olivia is taking respite in her quarters," I said, choking on that last word as Alex squeezed himself next to me in the doorway and poked his head in.

Liv looked up from her laptop, books spread around her on her bed, glasses perched on her nose—she only wore them around the apartment, opting for her contacts most of the time—her blond hair twisted up and held in place with a pencil.

Because she was my best friend for a very good reason, Liv played along, tipping up her nose and saying, "Greetings, good sir. Many welcomes and good tidings, cheerio." She gave a quick princess wave.

I stifled a giggle. The end could use some work, but I loved her for the effort.

Alex placed an arm behind him and bowed. The fact that he fit in with us so well was making it hard to remember I wasn't supposed to like him. Apparently I wasn't the only one who was already at ease with Alex's presence. Hammy vaulted onto Liv's bed and curled up at her feet, heaving a big sigh as her eyes fluttered closed.

I took Alex across the small hallway to my room.

"And here is the master suite." My accent faded. I bit my lip as I peered into my bedroom with the critical gaze of someone seeing a space they knew too well through someone else's eyes.

I suddenly felt self-conscious about the lights I'd crisscrossed above my bed, the wall of framed book quotes I'd collected over the years—Dad had gotten me one mostly every Christmas—and the Pinterest-inspired book lamp Maggie had made me for my twenty-first birthday. The way Alex's dark eyes roamed over my stuff with a full grin stretched across his face made my skin tingle, as if he were looking me up and down instead.

His gaze landed on the platform nine and three quarters sign I'd placed above the door to the bathroom. With a quick nod, he turned to me.

"Just what I'd expected."

I wasn't sure how I felt about him having expectations of my bedroom. It flustered me enough that I ended my haughty tour with a quick, "Um… bathroom's through there, if you need it."

Scuttling away from him, I plopped myself down in one of the squeaky chairs we'd placed around our small kitchen table. The list of suspects and clues Liv and I had created sat in the center, so I pulled it close to me and grabbed a pen from the cup sitting flush with the wall.

Alex settled across from me. "Nice place."

Swallowing, I said, "Thanks. Can I get you something to drink?"

He shook his head. "I'm good."

Tapping the pen against the table, I felt my nerves creep into my cheeks in hot waves. "Anyway, how 'bout this case?" I widened my eyes in a "crazy, huh?" kinda way. Then I pointed the pen down at the notepad. "So whatcha got?" My fingers wrestled the cap from the pen and my hand poised to write.

But Alex only shrugged. "Um… I think you know everything I know at this point."

I think my head did one of those quick, side-to-side double takes. "What?" The pen dropped from my fingers with a clatter.

"Yeah," he said with a nod, peering at the list in front of me, tilting his head a little to read it upside down.

"But… but…" I stammered.

He cocked an eyebrow at me.

"Your dad—he—you."

Alex shook his head. "Contrary to popular belief, police officers don't sit around eating doughnuts discussing crimes all day. I'm not on the case and he doesn't tell me much about his work."

Seemingly unconcerned about my stuttering, wide-eyed, openmouthed surprise, he pulled the notepad toward him and swiveled it around.

"But you were supposed to be getting inside information." My words sounded breathy, far away.

Alex's finger swung back and forth in front of me. "No, my job was to make sure you didn't get yourself in trouble. I never said I would get you classified information about the case."

He was right, of course. He hadn't. That had merely been my fervent hope, the reason I *told* myself I was keeping the guy around. Bouncing my knee under the table, I tried to think through the situation in which my brazen assumption had landed me.

"You mentioned *you* had new information, though?" Alex caught my eyes with his, quite a feat as they were rather dart-y and wild in my stupefaction.

In that moment, Flirty Alex was gone. Officer Alex took his place. His eyes scanned Liv's notes.

"I haven't heard anything about a…" he squinted at the notepad. "Naked Newt?" He cringed.

I waved a hand at him. "Oh, sorry. That's what we call Nate Newton, the guy who runs Bittersweet."

Alex's eyebrows shot up. "That guy? Definitely creepy. And you think he had something to do with this?"

"Not anymore." I shook my head. "He's cleared. We checked his alibi. Just normal creepy, not murder creepy."

Alex returned to the list. "Anything else?"

I felt the blood return to the rational, task-focused part of my brain.

"Uh, yeah. So my brother-in-law, Josh, works for NWU as a sound engineer and he hired Danny—er—the guy Stephanie mentioned her stepfather getting in a fight with during the sound check, remember?"

Alex nodded.

"Well, at first, Josh was adamant Danny was a good guy and couldn't have done anything, even though he took a break around the time Dr. C was killed."

"But?" Alex asked.

"Last night at dinner, he told me he was starting to doubt his insistence the guy was innocent." I went on to tell Alex all about Danny's motive and his access to the possible poison.

"And he hasn't told this to my dad?"

I shook my head.

He rubbed his hand across his chin, the rough skin of his fingers making a sandpaper sound as it sifted against his seven o'clock shadow. "Do you mind if I let the station know? They might want to talk to your brother-in-law again."

"Not at all." My spine straightened as an idea came to me. "*If* you find out something for me," I said.

"You're still on about that professor you hate?" He shook his head.

"I'm not 'on about' anything; I'm right. I know it." I pushed my shoulders back. "Look, you can tell your dad to bring in Josh for more questioning, but I want you to make sure he's taking Evensworth seriously as a suspect. I'm worried he's only looking into Fergie and potentially missing the actual killer."

A long sigh lifted Alex's chest. "I just have to make sure he's looking into him?"

Nodding emphatically, I said, "Yes. That's it." Then I tipped my head to the side. "And if you could find out if he has an alibi, that wouldn't hurt either."

He pushed air through his nose in a half laugh, half snort, but his eyes were squinted in what looked like amusement as he watched me. "Okay, Brooks. I'll see what I can do." Glancing down at his watch, he placed both hands on the table and stood up. "I'd better get going."

I followed him to the door.

As his fingers settled on the doorknob, he turned back toward me. "Don't do anything until I get back to you, okay?"

"With an alibi, right?" I bared my teeth in a smile.

"Right. No moving on any of this until I can confirm that."

"Or deny it." I put my hands up, palms out, to show how it was out of my hands if Evilsworth didn't have an alibi—which I was growing increasingly sure he didn't.

Alex chuckled. "Night, Pepper."

"Bye, Alex."

"See ya, Liv. See ya, Hot Dog," he called over me. And then—before I could chastise him for getting Hammy's name wrong again—he was gone.

I pushed out all of the breath I'd been holding along with the door until I heard it click shut. Then I threw the deadbolt until I heard it clunk into place.

18

Maggie convinced me to come over for lunch the next day. I had been dropping Hammy off at her place during the day while Liv and I went to our classes. She'd cornered me that morning, imploring me to come back during my break a few hours later. It was drizzly and gray and Mags was making homemade tomato soup and grilled cheese, so she didn't exactly have to twist my arm.

Which meant I entered the English building from a different wing as I headed for my last class of the day, Evilsworth's.

My stomach was full of warm comfort food, a fact I suddenly regretted as I rounded the corner into the main hallway. All of that food dropped to my knees as I saw Stephanie standing, cornered by Professor Evilsworth.

His back was to me and he was towering over the small woman, his deep voice too low for me to make out what he was saying. Stephanie's eyes frantically searched the hallway, then locked onto me. The light blue of her irises seemed to be draining, sucked dry with each new threat Evilsworth whispered to her.

Protectiveness surged up in my heart. As if to solidify her call for help, Stephanie flinched at the professor's last word.

"Stop that!" I called across the hallway.

It was pretty crowded; a good ten or fifteen other students milled around this beast and the sprite he'd trapped. *How stupid was he to threaten someone in public?* Evilsworth must've been operating solely on some sort of irrational rage brain. I could just imagine the Caliban curses slithering from his red lips...

A red plague rid you. Toads, beetles, bats light on you.

The monster spun around as my words splattered on his back, nearby students who'd been hit by the overspray of my exclamation turned to watch. Undeterred, I strode forward.

"How dare you talk to her." My finger flashed out like a switch blade and I pointed it at his heart.

Evilsworth's face, already red from their conversation, turned almost purple in his rage. Concern flashed across his face for a second, but the anger returned as I reached him and stopped.

"Haven't you put her through enough?" I snarled.

The man must've had a deep, untapped well of acting ability, because he continued to play dumb.

"Ms. Brooks, what on earth are you—?"

I would like to say I took a deep and measured breath, thought carefully about what I was going to say, and *then* shouted an accusation at the man in the middle of a mildly crowded hallway.

But no. Instead, I—

"What? Killing her father over your stupid book isn't enough? Now you've got to terrorize the woman even more?" Blood pounded in my ears. The hallway tilted.

Gasps sounded all around me. I couldn't tell if the gasps were of the *you're-so-right* kind or the *you're-so-crazy* kind because my eyes wouldn't leave Evilsworth.

His eyes grew wide and dark, and for a moment, I thought he was going to lunge toward me, offing me with a good ole strangle hold. *Those who threaten in public are likely to kill in public?* But after a moment his head jutted back.

"Brooks—you—what did you say?"

My finger, now less of a switchblade and more like a blade of grass, flailed between Stephanie and my professor. "You and her father fought about his review of your book right before he died. You hated him."

I scanned the faces of the other students in the hallway, resisting the urge to circle my hands in front of me in a "right, guys?" plea to garner their support when I saw their blank faces.

Evilsworth blinked and then nodded. "It's unfortunately true Davis and I had some heated words before he died." My professor jabbed a thumb back toward Stephanie. "That's actually what I was apologizing for." His large shoulders slumped and his bald head hung. "I regret how I let my temper get the best of me and that our last interaction was so... grievous." At this last word, he straightened back up to his normal, annoying height. "But I did *not* kill the poor man."

I took a deep breath and stood tall at my full height, too. "Oh yeah? Do you have an alibi, professor?" I hated how my voice wavered, how this teacher I hated seemed less and less like the sure-thing murderer I'd made him out to be in my mind.

His dark eyebrows lowered, casting a shadow over his eyes. "Not that it's any of your business, Ms. Brooks, but yes, I actually left campus right after my altercation with

Dr. Campbell to be there for the birth of my first grandchild."

The man pulled out his phone and swiped at the screen. He shoved the thing in my face and I saw him beaming, holding a tiny bundle.

"My daughter, my wife, my son-in-law, and pretty much the entire nursing staff at The Pine Crest Memorial Hospital can vouch I was there before the crime took place," he added.

I bit down on my bottom lip. The students milling about were whispering now, emboldened by the airtight alibi. I could only catch pieces of their conversations, but the ones I did left a terrible taste in my mouth.

"Crazy."

"So sad."

"Embarrassing."

"Who does she think she is?"

The hallway was my own personal amusement ride, flying around me too fast, making me want to puke. I tried to find Stephanie, but couldn't see her anymore, couldn't tell how she'd been affected by my presumptuous accusation.

Really, all I could seem to think was, *Alex is going to be so mad...*

Suddenly, a bony hand closed over my shoulder. I glanced down at the bright red polish and recognized Fergie's fingers grasping me.

"Pepper, darling, let's get you some tea." Her soft voice wrapped around me like the blue silk that draped off her arms, enveloping me as she steered me down the hallway and toward her office.

After a few quiet seconds, I croaked, "How much of that did you see?"

Her hand moved to pat my back and I knew—yep... she'd seen it all.

"My dear, you've been under a lot of stress this past year, what with losing your father." She tsked and pulled me tighter to her side as we walked into the lounge outside her office.

My gut churned at the reminder. Dad had been my compass, my equilibrium. He was the one I went to when I had a dilemma, always helping with his sage advice—and some well-timed quotes from the classics, of course. And without him, I felt lost. It was why I jumped into this major, it was the only piece of him I had left to cling to.

"I was so sure," I whispered, shaking my head as we walked down the corridor.

"Better three hours early than a minute too late." Was her reply.

I wanted to snort out a laugh. Fergie wasn't one to sugarcoat things and her Shakespeare quote was no different. Encouraging though it may sound, I remembered back to when the overzealous and paranoid Master Ford spoke those words in *The Merry Wives of Windsor*. She wanted me to feel better, but wasn't shy about telling me I'd acted irrationally.

Leading me into her office, Fergie sat me down in the chair in the corner. She shuffled off to make some tea, I assumed, hearing the electric water kettle begin to sizzle.

Groaning, I let my face fall straight into my open palm. *What had I done?*

I'd been so headstrong about being able to do something on my own, I hadn't even stopped to think if I should. Alex had told me not to act until I heard from him and I'd gone and accused someone. *Maybe Alex won't find out.* I inwardly snorted. *Yeah, right.* On this campus, in this town...

Somewhere in the clutter of Fergie's office, I heard the

kettle click off and water pour into a mug. Seconds later, there was a cup of Earl Gray steaming in front of me, the lovely citrus scent of bergamot soothing my whirling mind.

I let my eyes drift closed and pulled the cup toward me, about to take a steaming sip.

"Let it steep a little longer, dear," Fergie said quietly.

Wrapping my fingers around the warm mug, I lowered it to my lap. And as Fergie tutted around me, busy with this and that, I sat there in silence. I'm sure Fergie was just giving me space, but I couldn't help but use the time to close my eyes and replay my terrible hallway accusation over and over in my head.

I don't know how many minutes went by, but I realized the mug in my hand had grown colder and I went to take a sip. But as the first drops lighted on my tongue, I pulled back and squeezed my face into a scowl, jolted back into reality by the bitter drink.

Fergie, looked up from the paper she was reading and her face flattened as she watched me. "Oh, I'm sorry. Your first try was too soon and now I fear we've let it steep too long. Would you like me to make a new one?"

I wrinkled my nose, but shook my head. "No. I'm fine. This is good. I'll take it slow."

Setting the cup on top of the nearest bookshelf, I took a deep, calming breath. Which was when I noticed—*Holy mother of messes!*—Fergie's office was an absolute disaster. I was used to her questionable "piles and stacks" system of organization, but this was downright chaos.

My wide eyes took in the papers everywhere, books laid upon books, and trinkets littering the floor, then they landed on Fergie.

"What happened in here?" I felt slightly bad about the

incredulity lacing my words. The woman had just saved me from a public death by humiliation, after all.

Fergie looked like she was going to wave a dismissive hand toward me, but instead the hand got lost fumbling through her wispy waves of hair and she grimaced as she surveyed the scene.

"Ah, yes. They brought me a new desk and chair. I got everything out of the old one, but… lost my way sometime after that."

My heart ached for her. She was scattered at the best of times. Trying to reorganize her whole desk in a time like this was a recipe for disaster.

"Here, let me help you." I stood, motioning to the desk and the piles.

Fergie let her head sway back and forth. "Oh, no. I don't even know where I'm going. You don't want to follow me down that winding, possibly unending path. You're not even my TA. I couldn't ask that of you."

This woman had done so much to help me. It was the least I could do to help her with this. Sure, I wasn't a master at organization—Liv might argue I was as bad as Fergie, or worse—but I could do this.

"Look, my next class is Evensworth's and I'm most definitely not going—at least not today. This will help me take my mind off of what happened in the hall back there." I gave her a pleading look.

Dipping her head in concession, she said, "Okay. Thank you, dear."

I rubbed my hands together. "Where do we start?"

Fergie sighed. "I suppose finding a common thread and following it through."

Nodding, I plopped down on the floor, next to the largest stack of papers. "I can do that."

The new wooden desk was nice, classic and sensible. I leaned over until I could reach the largest drawer, then pulled it open to see what kind of storage we were working with. *Oh good. Hanging files. I could definitely work with these.*

As I dove into the first stack, Fergie pulled up a stool and sat with a grunt. "Would you like me to add some water to this?" she asked, picking up the cup of tea and setting it on the desk in front of me.

Oh, right. I had all but forgotten. There was a large part of me that didn't really want any more of the bitter concoction, but I also didn't want to be rude.

"No, thanks." I grimaced out a smile then reached forward, pinched the delicate handle with my thumb and pointer finger, and tipped it warily to my lips.

After a few sips, however, I either got used to the intensity or most of my taste buds had jumped ship, because it started to taste normal. Getting back to work, I let my mind wrap around the task in front of me and the incident with Evilsworth melted away.

A FEW HOURS LATER, I sat in relatively the same place on the floor. The space around me, however, had changed dramatically. I'd set Fergie up with a folder for each class in which to keep her copies and syllabi and then a few others for things such as "papers to sign" and "play pamphlets."

Fergie had left a few minutes ago to go grab us some dinner. Even though we'd made good headway, we still had a good hour or two of work left. Liv had texted, too.

"Going to the football game tonight with Carson. Wanna come?"

My fingers hovered over my screen, wanting desperately to tell Liv all about my terrible blunder with Evilsworth, but

Literally Dead

it would take a whole lot of typing. I didn't want to ruin her time with Carson, either. She must really like the guy if she was willing to go to a sporting event with him. What Liv knew about sports could fit on a grain of rice—not that I was any better.

I typed, "*No thanks! I'm having dinner with Fergie. Will be home later.*"

The NWU Marmots were one of the worst college teams in the state and most of the games they played only served to add to the embarrassment. Plus, I was enjoying how this organizing project had kept my mind off the incident and I desperately wanted to lose myself in that concentration again.

I texted Maggie, asking if she could watch Hammy for a few more hours. When she confirmed it was no problem, I put my phone behind me and headed into the next pile. I came across some more copies, these for her Shakespeare studies classes. I placed them in the stack I'd started. But under those I found something that didn't fit any of the files I'd already created.

A worn, ancient-looking Pee-Chee folder, stuffed almost to the point of busting, sat on top of the stack. I grabbed it and flipped it open. My face pulled into a grin. Inside the left pocket were a few yellowed essays that must've been typed on an actual typewriter. They were Fergie's, from when she'd been in university at Oxford.

Licking my lips in anticipation, I flipped open the first, about her analysis of *Moby Dick*. Oh my gosh, this was like gold. I loved reading young Fergie's crisp and concise writing. I could see right away how she'd made a name for herself so quickly in this field.

Sliding that paper back into the pocket, I turned my attention to the right side. This one held multiple envelopes, but they were the square-ish kind which usually held cards, instead of the long, business variety.

My fingers curled into a fist mid reach. I glanced at the door to Fergie's office. She'd closed it on her way out. I didn't want to be invasive, but what could it hurt to look?

Opening the oldest-looking one first and unfolding the crackly paper inside, I was met with a page full of small, scrawling script. It started with *Dear Sharon*, at the top. My eyes scanned to the bottom and I inhaled as I read, *Love, Davis*.

My mind was a swirl of excitement and worry. I so desperately wanted to know more about Fergie and Dr. Campbell's relationship, but I also didn't want to pry into her personal life too much.

Just a peek couldn't hurt. Right?

My eyes pored over the words and my heart ached as I read Dr. Campbell's declarations of love for my beloved professor. They were young and mad about each other. So much so, he *knew* they would be fine as he finished his doctoral thesis in England and she moved back to the States where she'd gotten a job teaching at Northern Washington University.

Folding it carefully, I tucked the letter back into its envelope and pulled out the next in the pocket. I know I said I wouldn't pry, but now I was a girl who knew the beginning and end of a love story and I needed to figure out the middle. *What had happened with them?*

Out of the twenty-or-so envelopes tucked into the pocket, I pulled out the next in line, also showing its age in color and wear. My heart broke as I read this one, dated almost two years later. Everything became clear. Dr. Campbell assured Fergie he was very happy for her and, no, he didn't hold any resentment toward her for falling in love with Ben. One couldn't help who they fell in love with. It was probably better this way.

Fergie had broken it off, had met someone new. My fingers worked quickly, putting that letter away and pulling out another.

I blinked at the date of the next one, and the crisp whiteness of the paper. Dr. C had written this one just last year. Those two had kept up writing letters, even beyond their relationship. Gulping, I read on.

And I felt sick.

Dearest Sharon,

I'm so sorry, but I cannot do this. Never in my life did I think I would become an adulterer. Just writing that word makes me wish for a quick end. Mary needs me right now more than ever. I was a fool to forget that.

Best, Davis

Toads. Beetles. Bats.

Dr. Campbell and Fergie were having an affair? While his wife was dying? And he'd called it off.

Heat coated my throat and my tongue tasted bitter, metallic. No, it couldn't be. I shook my head, wanted to run away from the doubt. But the problem was, with this new information, there wasn't much doubt left.

What if I'd been terribly wrong? What if Fergie wasn't merely an old flame, but a scorned lover? That would mean the police were right. Dr. Ferguson *had* killed Davis Campbell.

The letter crinkled in my hands as they began to shake.

I needed to get out of there. Detective Valdez needed to see this letter. I scrambled to my feet.

But the door opened and Fergie blocked my escape.

19

When I was six, our dog, Buttons, had found a bunny in the yard. His instincts had kicked in and he'd grabbed the thing by the neck when it tried to dart away. And while he hadn't bitten down, the bunny had died—from a heart attack, my dad had explained. It had been *so* scared, its heart had stopped.

I hadn't fully understood how it could happen until that moment, standing in front of Fergie. My fingers, giving up, let go of the letter and it wafted to the floor. Her eyes narrowed as they slid from my twitchy eyes to the open folder.

"Pepper, darling." Her voice was sweet, as it always was when she spoke to me. But for the first time, I felt like it was an act, like she was merely playing out a scene. A villain luring in another victim.

In her hands, she clutched a paper bag from the sandwich shop on campus. My eyes cut to my phone, where I'd left it on the floor. *Dammit.* I tried to calculate the possibility of grabbing it and running. She wasn't a young woman. True, I didn't work out, but surely I was faster than…

My mouth went dry as I remembered the tea.

The bitter taste. Fergie moving the cup closer, reminding me to drink.

The room tilted and my face grew hot. She'd poisoned me, too. My hand raked at my throat. *Oh my god. Was I already dying? Was it already too late?* My heart raced in a way I'd never experienced before.

"For goodness sake, Pepper. What happened?" She took a step toward me.

My hand shot up, trembling as I held it out in front of myself. "No. Don't—don't come any closer."

Fergie's face darkened. Her eyes flashed to the letter again.

"I read it." The words flew out of me before I could stop them. "I know you were having an affair, that he put a stop to it." A weight settled on my chest. I shouldn't be talking to her. I needed to run. I needed to get the police.

But there was too big a part of my heart needing to know the truth.

I'd trusted her.

Dr. Campbell had trusted her.

"Why'd you do it, Fergie?" Tears crowded my eyes.

Her fire-engine-red mouth dropped open. "Pepper, I—" She stepped forward again.

"No!" I sobbed. "I'll scream. There has to be someone close." I pointed to the hallway behind her. *Was there?* Classes were over for the day and darkness crept in through the window in Fergie's office.

Feeling momentarily hopeless, I whispered, "How long do I have? Is it at least quick?" I swallowed the seventeen other questions lining my throat.

Fergie shook her head. "I don't know what you're talking about, dear."

"The poisoned tea. Just like you gave him. Hebanon. Like *Hamlet*." My accusing eyes drilled into hers.

Her eyes flitted back and forth around the room: to me, the tea cup, the letter, back to me. Oh, the woman really was made for the stage. Even when she was finally cornered, she still managed to act as if she were none the wiser.

"Pepper," she said carefully. "You believe I did this?" There was a practiced sadness pushing her words forward.

I swallowed and nodded.

"Because you found a letter from Davis breaking it off with me?"

I nodded again.

The older woman closed her eyes. Her blue eyeshadow was so bright in the florescent lights of the office. Or maybe the poison was distorting my mind, a sign it was about to take me.

She opened her eyes finally, a calm smile lifting her features. Fergie dipped her chin, gesturing to the folder of letters at my feet. "Before you run to the police. Would you please locate a white envelope with a butterfly stamp on it?"

Licking my lips, I narrowed my eyes at her. What was she playing at?

"Go ahead. Right in there." She pointed.

Unsure I even had enough time to get to the police before the poison took affect, I figured I might at least use my last few moments to find out where she was going with this.

I kept my eyes on her as I knelt. My fingers splayed the remaining letters out on the floor until I found the one she was talking about. I picked up the envelope she mentioned, but also grabbed my phone before standing up, holding it out to show her I could call someone at any moment if this didn't go where I liked.

Fergie nodded somberly.

Slipping the phone in my pocket, so I could use both hands, I unfolded the requested letter. It was of different handwriting, the cursive letters fatter and taller than Dr. Campbell's low scrawl. It was dated last year as well.

Sharon,

I should call, but I'm honestly not sure my voice would hold, nor am I positive I'd be able to say what I need to say as eloquently as I might through this pen. I've always loved Davis' stories about how you two maintained written correspondence even in an increasingly paperless world.

The long and short of it is: I'm dying. I have been for years and can see it taking such a toll on my dear Davis. It's possible I'll go tomorrow. It's possible I'll hang on for another ten years. This cancer may be killing my body, but it would kill my soul to know I've held Davis back from happiness. I've already talked to him about this, but I want him to move on, to start his new life, the rest of his life.

And I hope he does that with you.

He and I have had an amazing love, but I know you've always been in his heart. You have my blessing. Life is short. Start the rest of yours as soon as you can. You never know how much, or little, time you have left.

"If I can stop one heart from breaking, I shall not live in vain"

Mary

My heartbeat pulsed, making my body sway with each new pump.

"She gave you permission? Wanted you to be together?" I croaked, looking up to meet Fergie's pained gaze.

The woman nodded. "We never did, however. Davis, fortunately, was much stronger than I. That letter you found from him came in response to one I wrote… in essence asking if he would have me, if I could move to England and be with him." She sighed. "Don't get me wrong, I loved Ben."

I remembered meeting Fergie's tall husband before he'd passed about ten years ago. He had a booming laugh and always seemed to wear Fergie on his arm like a prize.

A tear rolled down her cheek. "He had my body and my heart, that man. But Davis always had my mind. And the thought I could spend the rest of my days with him, quoting Shakespeare and discussing literary theory was enough of a temptation. I even applied for a job at Oxford last year, before receiving that letter from him."

"It turned out for the best anyway," she continued. "That was right around the time when your father..." her voice cracked and she shook her head, leaving the sentence unfinished. "I'm so glad I could be here for you through that." Her eyes were soft, caring, loving.

My mind reeled. I was so confused. This didn't seem like an act.

I pulled in a deep breath. "So you didn't kill him?"

Fergie shook her head. "I was hoping we might be able to start that life together, now Mary had really gone. It's why I invited him out here. Alas..."

"And you didn't poison me?" I noticed my throat no longer felt hot.

More head shaking. "I promise, it was just over-steeped Earl Gray. Unpalatable, but not deadly."

It felt like a weight lifted off my chest and I pulled in a deep breath. As I released it, my shoulders slumped forward, tired of the tension and the taut position in which I'd been holding myself.

Now that I wasn't watching her through the paranoid lens of accusation, she transformed back into my kind mentor. Her wrinkled face pulled into a sad smile. Nancy

Drew would probably not have approved of what I did next, but... letting Mary's letter flutter to the floor, I stepped forward and pulled Fergie into a hug.

"I'm sorry I thought you were a murderer." My words were muffled by her long blue scarf.

Her bony arms wrapped around me and she patted my back. "It's quite alright, dear. This has been difficult, to say the least."

Pulling back, I blinked. "But if Evensworth didn't do it... and you didn't do it... then it must've been Danny."

I was suddenly furious with myself for not making him more of a priority, for not questioning him yet. I just hoped the police had talked to Josh again.

Wait. The police.

"We need to let Detective Valdez know Danny's the killer," I said. My muscles tightened and I pushed away from Fergie.

"Hold on there, dear." Fergie grabbed onto my arm.

My body wanted to spin out of there, needed to move. My forehead creased in question. "We can clear your name. Why hold on?"

Fergie's face softened. "Pepper, you've accused two souls of taking another today because you jumped to conclusions. Shall we think this through? Make sure you've got the right person this time?"

Chewing on my bottom lip, I nodded. The woman had a good point.

Fergie walked over to her desk, pushed aside the last remaining piles, and pulled up another chair. "How about you tell me over dinner why you think this Danny person killed him. Then, if the evidence is sufficient, we can head to see Detective Valdez together."

My soup and sandwich at Maggie's had been hours ago and I could feel my stomach rumble at the thought of food.

"Okay." I plopped into the chair next to her and we ate while I told her everything.

FERGIE CRUNCHED DOWN ON A PICKLE, her eyes wandering along the ceiling as she contemplated what I'd told her.

"It does sound like he'd have access to multiple options. Both Poison Hemlock and Western Water Hemlock grow around here. Even the motive is believable. People have killed for less." Fergie sighed. "What I can't make sense of is how he got the poison *into* Davis."

I nodded. That was where I was getting hung up, too. Before I could say anything, however, my phone buzzed with a text. It was Alex. I groaned.

"Where are you?"

There weren't any emojis or an abundance of punctuation, but I could feel the tension lacing those words. He must've heard about my public hallway accusation. I glanced up at Fergie.

"Any chance you think I could hide out in here forever?" I let out a strangled laugh.

Fergie patted my hand with hers. "The web of our life is of a mingled yarn, good and ill together."

That Shakespeare quote was as good as Fergie telling me I needed to take care of what I'd created, not run away from it.

I nodded and I texted back.

"In Professor Ferguson's office."

A few seconds later, his response popped up.

"Meet me at the library. Now."

Oh boy. I was definitely in trouble. No need to read into that one.

Exhaling, I slapped my hands down on my thighs. "Well, I need to go deal with the ill-yarn I've—er—knit?"

"You do that, dear." Fergie cleaned up our empty sandwich wrappers and placed them in the garbage. "I'll keep working here."

Grabbing my bag, I stopped at the door. "I can come back later and help you finish up."

She waved a hand. "Nonsense. You got me started. That's all I needed. I'll be done here in no time."

I sighed and turned to leave. Even if she didn't need me, it would be a good excuse to keep my meeting with Alex as short as possible.

The night had fully wrapped its indigo robes around Pine Crest and the NWU campus by the time I stepped out into the chilly evening. Campus was eerily quiet. Sure, it was closing in on seven, but there were usually students milling about here and there. Tonight I didn't see a soul in the span between the English building and the library. *Where was everyone?*

My brain pulled up the memory of Liv's text in answer to my question. *The football game.* Of course. Campus Creek trickled under my feet as I stopped for a moment on the small footbridge, taking in the delicious silence before I subjected myself to the scolding I knew was coming. My lungs full of cool air and my resolve steeled, I walked forward.

Alex was waiting for me outside the library. My heart skipped slightly as I saw his eyes light up when they landed on me. He held two steaming to-go cups in his hands and strode forward.

Huh… He didn't look angry. In fact, he seemed—

"I'm so relieved to see you," he sighed out the words and held the coffee toward me. Its swirling steam smelled heavenly, like caramel and chocolate.

"It's decaf," Alex said, tipping his head to the dark sky. "Other than that, the creepy guy in the coffee shop said it was your favorite—something ridiculous I can't remember."

My fingers made grabby motions at the cup. "A creamy caramel mocha pie latte?" I curled my hands around the warm drink and took a quick sip. "Oh… yummmmm."

I was in total warm-tummy, shoulders-pulled-up-high happiness when the conspiracy theory part of my brain woke up again. My eyes flashed to Alex's relieved face.

"What's this for?" I asked. "And why are you so relieved to see me?"

Alex's dark eyes held me, then so did his hand squeezing my shoulder. "Pepper, don't be mad. I needed the coffee as bait. I wasn't sure how much convincing I would need to get you to come to me."

Pulse racing again, I lowered the drink and asked, "Why?"

"I need you to stay away from her." He still hadn't removed his hand. "I spent all day at the station."

So that's why he didn't know about my embarrassing public accusation of Evilsworth.

His voice dropped low and serious. "It's her. Dad's almost positive. They're waiting for a test to come back from the lab and he's going to make the arrest."

"Arrest Fergie? That's ridiculous," I said with a surprising amount of astonishment for a person who'd accused the woman of the same crime only an hour before.

I shoved the cup back toward him and smacked his hand off my shoulder. "Here, I don't want your stupid delicious bait coffee. I know she didn't do it."

Alex's jaw ticked, but he didn't take the cup. "She did and you're in danger, too. Or do you not remember the threatening note she left you when she broke into your place yesterday?"

I blinked, shaking my head. "No. I just spent hours with her. She could've killed me so many times if she'd wanted." I decided not to mention the "poisoned" Earl Gray tea incident.

There was so much I needed to catch Alex up on, but there was no time if the police were preparing to arrest Fergie. I needed to figure out this case, quickly.

"What finally convinced your dad it was her?" I asked.

Alex leaned in close, even though there was no one near. "She and Dr. C were having an affair. One *he* ended," he said, punctuating the point with an eyebrow raise.

"No," I shook my head. I wanted to tell him they'd never gone through with it, how Fergie had been fine with it, relieved even. But something was bugging me too much to focus on explaining it to Alex. The letters were still in Fergie's office. The police hadn't taken them…

"How'd you find out about that?" I asked, but right as the question left my lips, I knew the answer. "Oh my gosh. I know who killed Dr. Campbell." My whole body tingled as everything clicked into place. Unlike the last time I'd said this sentence in front of Alex, this time I was sure.

Alex nodded. "…Yeah…Dr. Ferguson… like I told y—"

"No." I dropped my coffee, ignoring the splash as it hit the ground as I grabbed onto his jacket with both hands. I rolled wild eyes at him as I said, "We need to go find Fergie. She's in trouble."

20

Alex didn't respond in the action-man, let's-go-save-her way I'd hoped for. Instead, he stood there and blinked down at the spilled coffee dripping all over our shoes and puddling on the sidewalk.

"I *have* to go to her," I said as I let go of his jacket and walked backward. "I'm sorry."

Alex's face was dark and his jaw looked so tight I was afraid he might crack a few molars. But after a groan and a quick pat to get some of the coffee off his previously clean jeans, he followed me.

I wheeled around and started to jog. I heard Alex do so, too. My school bag bounced at my side awkwardly, making my already-out-of-practice gait even more ungainly.

"It's not that Evensworth guy," he said, pulling up level with me. I noticed his coffee was gone, too. "His alibi checked out. Pepper, it's Professor Ferguson. I'm sorry."

I shook my head. I already knew it wasn't Evilsworth, but didn't have time to tell him how. Right now, I needed to make sure I was right.

"The poisonous plant used…" I said as I ran, pausing to suck in air—Liv was right, I really needed to work out more.

"Yeah?" Alex asked.

"I'm guessing it was something like Hemlock?" I glanced back at him.

"Cicutoxin." He nodded. "Western Water Hemlock."

I shook my head and laughed. It wasn't a happy laugh, more like the "how could I have been so stupid and blind?" kind.

We pulled up in front of the English building. The lights illuminating the facade gave the white stone an ominous appearance. A shiver raked its way down my back despite my sweaty state. My chest heaved, painful after pulling in too much cold air, but I couldn't wait any longer for my breath to catch up with us. Fergie needed me.

"So you think it might be Danny? The sound guy?" Alex asked as we pulled open the doors.

The warm air inside the English building washed over us as we pulled open the doors and headed down the hallway, our sneakers squeaking as we ran over the tiles.

"No." The hallways flew past us in a blur. "It had to be someone he knew well, whom he trusted." I shot the words over to Alex. "I think the poison was in a tea made from the roots. Danny may have had access to the plants, but he couldn't have gotten them into Dr. C," I added, my side starting to cramp.

Screeching to a stop outside Fergie's office, I grimaced and leaned forward, trying to hear anything that might clue us into what we were walking into. When I couldn't make out any sounds, I threw open the door—I'd seen the police do it in movies and figured it might give us the element of surprise.

But the room was empty. My stomach plummeted.

Literally Dead

"No, no, no." I walked forward. "She was just here." I turned to look at Alex who looked unconcerned.

"Maybe she's in the bathroom?" He shrugged and then, under his breath, added, "Or running away because she knows she's been caught."

I shook my head and turned away from him. That's when my gaze caught on a piece of paper on her desk. Jumping forward, I grabbed at it.

"Oh no." My face flushed hot and cold as I read over the familiar handwriting.

There is a willow grows aslant a brook,
That shows his hoar leaves in the glassy stream;
There with fantastic garlands did I come
Of crow-flowers, nettles, daisies, and long purples
That liberal shepherds give a grosser name,
But our cold maids do dead men's fingers call them:
There, on the pendent boughs my coronet weeds
Clambering to hang, an envious sliver broke;
When down my weedy trophies and myself
Fell in the weeping brook. My clothes spread wide;
And, mermaid-like, awhile they bore me up:
Which time I chanted snatches of old tunes;
As one incapable of my own distress,
Or like a creature native and indued
Unto that element: but long it could not be
Till that my garments, heavy with their drink,
Pull'd the poor wretch from my melodious lay
To muddy death.

I shoved it toward Alex.

His eyes scanned it, then he lowered the paper. "Again, your theory about the poison tea only solidifies the fact it was her. This sounds like she knew she was done for and she's running away." He checked the paper again and his forehead creased. "Or something more depressing."

"Yeah, like suicide." I shook my head.

For the first time, Alex's jaw began to tighten in concern. I saw him straighten as I pulled the paper away from him again.

"This is Queen Gertrude telling Laertes about his sister Ophelia's death. Only this version has *I* and *my* in place of *she* and *her*. They wanted it to read like a suicide note. Just like Dr. C's." I scoffed. "What the murderer doesn't know is Fergie is a literature purist and would never do such a thing, even if she were going to commit suicide."

Alex pressed his lips together and breathed out through his nose. "Which means?"

"Fergie doesn't have much time." I closed my eyes and started listing things aloud, brainstorming. "Ophelia drowned after climbing the tree, the branch breaking, and then falling in. She gets caught and drowns." I snapped my fingers and opened my eyes. "I think I know where they are."

I raced for the door, the fake suicide note fluttering in my hand, but I stopped, pivoted, and ran back to grab a letter from the pile on the floor. Then I ducked out from under the strap of my school bag and dumped it on the floor. Now I was ready to run. I nodded to Alex and we sped down the hallway.

Alex's forehead was forming deeper and deeper creases as he matched my pace. "So if it isn't Danny, and you swear it wasn't Fergie…"

After accusing two people already tonight, I decided to ask one more question. "Who told your dad about the affair?"

Alex's eyes locked onto me in a way that made me

worried he wasn't looking where he was running. "Stephanie, but…" His brown eyes darkened as he finally appeared to be taking me seriously. He picked up the pace.

We threw our bodies at the exterior doors of the English building and ran out into the cold. I led Alex to the path that would take us behind the science building. The botany greenhouses were close to there, too. At one point, I saw a light flash in Alex's hand. We reached the bridge crossing over the creek by the willow and the sight that met me stopped me in my tracks.

A body floated face up in the water near the bank. Long, draped blue fabric swirling in the water's ghostly eddies.

I gasped. "No." The word was a whisper on my lips. Tears jumped into my eyes.

A dark shape moved next to me in my blurred vision. Swiping at my eyes, I made out Alex's form crossing the rest of the bridge and heading down the hill. Sniffling, I ran after him.

The ground was slick from an afternoon rain, so he had to lean back and pick his way carefully down to the water. The creek trickled merrily in the background, bubbling by in a way which suggested it had no idea the sadness it held.

Alex reached her first and plunged into the knee-high waters, wrapping his arms around the billowing blue fabric. He lifted and pulled her out until she was out of the water then bent down to check her pulse. I was by her side in a second, slipping in the mud as I grasped onto her cold hand, waiting. Alex's dark eyes shone in the moonlight as they met mine.

"She still has a pulse." He smiled and then pulled out his phone. "I'm going to call for help."

"No. You're not." The chilling words made my spine straighten. I glanced up, gripping Fergie's hand protectively.

Stephanie's small form was easy to miss next to the large willow tree. That same long, blue button-up she'd worn the first time we'd met flapped in the breeze. But while she looked like the same person I'd met in that hallway, her voice was different. Gone was the small bird, the delicate whispers.

And then there was the gun she was pointing at us. That definitely hadn't been there before either.

"Step away from her." Her voice shook with anger.

My eyes cut back to Alex who still had yet to put his phone away. He didn't look at me, though, his gaze was trained on Stephanie.

"Please!" I cried out. "She's dying. She needs help." Tears spilled down my cheeks as I scooted closer to Fergie's body, slipping on the muddy bank.

Ignoring me, Stephanie said, "Put the phone *away*." She didn't yell, but there was a blood-curdling craziness distorting each word.

As much as her tone sent a cold chill deep into my bones, it didn't seem to faze Alex, whose voice cut through the darkness. "Just calm down. We can talk this through."

"Yeah, let's do that," she chided. "Talk it through. How might it go? Poor guilty Sharon knew she'd been caught when the nosy TA and her boyfriend started to figure things out. She couldn't have any survivors, so she shot them before taking the same poison she fed to her *lover*." Stephanie spat out that last part.

My mind reeled. *Of course.* That's why she'd done all of this. That's why she'd put a warning in Fergie's purse after Dr. Campbell had been killed. Stephanie must've found out about Fergie and Davis. But… found out what? They hadn't *actually* gone through with any of it.

"Stephanie, they didn't do it. They didn't have an

affair!" I blurted out, hating how small my voice sounded, how it shook from fear.

She snorted. "Sure they didn't. And the two-week trip he took to America before Mom died had *nothing* to do with that letter that home-wrecker sent him." She shook her head. "She was dying and that lying bastard couldn't wait until her body was even cold to go running to *her*." She pointed the gun at Fergie's prone body next to me.

Each breath felt ragged as I pulled it into my lungs.

"The trip didn't have anything to do with her. Davis ended the affair before it even started." I spoke fast, letting the words spill out. I could feel Alex stiffen next to me in warning, hoping I knew where I was going with this. "Stephanie, your mother *wanted* them to move on, together."

She laughed in response and stepped closer.

I could see movement in the distance, lights from flashlights. The football game must be over. And while a crowd could mean hope for us, it could just as easily mean more victims for Stephanie to shoot.

My heart hammered. I didn't have time to explain everything. Fergie didn't have time. I gripped the letter I'd pulled from the pile on the floor, having almost forgotten I had it. Maybe if she could hear it from her mother…

"I have proof," I called out, holding the letter up. "Your mom wrote to Professor Ferguson."

Assumption guided my trembling fingers in the silence which followed. I opened the letter, cursing the darkness and fumbling as my muddy fingers marred the white paper. Tipping it toward the light, I read her mother's letter aloud in one breath, until I reached the quote at the end. "If I can stop one heart from breaking, I shall not live in vain."

I heard a small gasp.

I remembered Stephanie saying how much her mother

loved Emily Dickinson. After staring at the white paper, my eyes took a moment to adjust and Stephanie was a denim-colored blur as my eyes searched the darkness.

"She asked for this?" Stephanie's voice sounded crushed.

Alex hadn't been reading off a stark white piece of paper and didn't seem to be having the same problem as me in the seeing-in-the-dark department. The moment a distraught Stephanie's hands drifted slightly lower, Alex pounced forward. He had the gun in his hands before I could blink.

Stephanie didn't seem to care. She curled up and crumpled into a sobbing heap, mumbling words I couldn't make out.

Just then, flashlight beams cut through the darkness, making us throw our hands up to shield our eyes.

"Alex, you okay?"

I scolded myself for ever thinking Detective Valdez's deep voice sounded harsh or cold. No, it was the most wonderful, comforting, warm sound in the world. I almost cried out in relief.

There was an audible rush of air from Alex before he said, "Yeah." I could tell he felt relieved as well. "Did you bring the paramedics? Professor Ferguson's been given something. She's alive, but in pretty bad shape."

Dropping the letter, one of my hands latched onto Fergie's freezing fingers again while I pressed the other to her cold cheek. *Was it the darkness or was her chest not moving anymore?*

"Boys, down here. Quick," Detective Valdez barked.

All around us bodies raced, orders were called out and followed, a big spotlight was propped on the bridge to help light the area as they worked. Alex's dad walked down, taking the gun from his son and clapping him into a tight hug for a second before tipping his head to me and then handcuffing Stephanie.

I watched with wide eyes and a worried heart as they took Fergie away on a stretcher, the red and white lights of the ambulance flashing as it sped away, over the campus grass and footpaths.

My body began to shake in the cold, dark letdown. But right as I feared I might collapse, steady arms wrapped around me and a broad chest supported my head. I leaned back and closed my eyes. Safe.

21

Entering the library, I paused briefly in the foyer to close my umbrella and breathe in the calming smell. I usually didn't use an umbrella, but it was pouring buckets outside and my jacket was still all muddy from the other night down by the creek. I sighed, propping the umbrella against the wall next to a few others, then strode forward, pulling the thin book out from under my wool sweater where I'd been keeping it safe from the rain.

Ginger was sitting at the circulation desk and she smiled up at me when I slipped the book into the "returns" slot. The opening dumped into a cart hidden under the desk and I watched Ginger's eyes flit down into the pile. Her eyebrows rose.

"Are the rumors true, then?" She reached down and picked up the copy of *The Tragedy of Hamlet: Prince of Denmark*.

My cheeks flushed. It had only been two days. I suppose things did spread quickly in this town, though. Detective Valdez's stern voice repeated in my mind, warning me not to discuss the case or he'd toss me in jail along with Stephanie.

"Um... what? I don't know what you're referring to." I backed away from the counter.

Ginger stood, mouth open as if she were about to ask another question I couldn't answer.

"Sorry, I—gotta go find something!" I spun around and bolted for the spiral staircase, fingers grasping the railing as I used it to pull myself up and away from her.

Safely upstairs, I strode toward the Shakespeare aisle. After being so close to a real-life tragedy, I needed to read one of his comedies. Desperately. I wanted people joking, playing tricks on one another, and only *pretending* to be dead. *A little romance wouldn't hurt either,* I thought as I rounded the corner.

And stopped dead in my tracks.

A familiar tall, dark, and seriously handsome figure stood in front of the Shakespeare section, dark eyebrows furrowed as he paged through a book. He glanced up as I skidded to a stop, quickly shoving the book he'd been reading back onto the shelf. I grimaced as I watched one of the pages bend backwards, caught in the fast, careless movement.

"Ah!" I shot forward, fingers reaching. Snatching the book, I smoothed its poor bent pages back into place and glared up at Alex. "I cannot believe you work here with the way you bully books." I tsked and shook my head.

Alex didn't seem to take my scolding seriously, though, because he was grinning at me like some sort of fantastic-looking fool. "It's good to see you."

I breathed through the tightness in my chest. "You, too."

We hadn't seen each other since the other night. The

past forty-eight hours had been some sort of cruel whirlwind, like someone had put my life on a super spin cycle.

"I was going to stop by, but I figured you'd probably be with Fergie." He cleared his throat and ran a hand through his dark hair.

I nodded. I had spent the last day at the hospital, curled uncomfortably in a torturous chair, listening to the sweet, sweet sound of her breathing. She hadn't woken up until hour thirteen, and by that time her kids had flown in and the room had gotten a little crowded, so I'd headed home.

Maggie had called our mom after hearing from me that night. My lawyer mother had spun into town early the next morning, cutting her business trip a day short. I'd only been allotted a small window free from her litigious grasp to come drop off my library book because I'd told her it would be late otherwise—my mother was without-a-doubt the source of my ingrained sense of rule-following.

"Fergie's family is here now," I told Alex.

"My dad says she's doing well." Alex watched me as if he were worried I might report otherwise.

I nodded. "She's doing great. Thanks to you."

I tried not to think about how close we'd come to losing her. Luckily, Stephanie had proven to be a true botanist below all of that anger and angst, and had wanted to try out a different poison with Fergie than she had with Dr. Campbell. She'd swapped that quick-acting Western Water Hemlock, for its slower-acting cousin, plain old Poison Hemlock.

If she hadn't wanted so badly to observe how the different poisons affected her victims, the stomach pump and IV probably wouldn't have been enough. I shivered at the thought.

It hadn't hurt that we had found her so quickly. Or that

Alex had sent his dad our location as we'd been running toward the willow.

Alex shook his head. "You're the real hero. I think my dad is secretly impressed."

I chuckled. "If he is, he's burying it pretty darn deep." The stoic detective had seemed like he was about to burst a blood vessel when I'd recounted everything I'd done before leaving the station. "He wasn't very happy about all of the accusing."

Alex smiled. "To do a great right, do a little wrong."

Gasping at the quote, I looked at the book Alex had been holding—*The Merchant of Venice*. A smirk tugged at the corner of my mouth as I met his gaze. "You read it?"

He nodded. "I wanted to see what all of this Shakespeare hype was about." He motioned to the paperback. "I picked it because I liked the sound of the whole 'pound of flesh' part."

"And?" I asked.

"It wasn't bad," he conceded. "That Shylock guy was pretty awesome."

I scoffed. "Shylock? Portia gives one of the most beautiful speeches in all of literature during the trial and you remember stab-happy Shylock?"

Alex's hand landed on my shoulder. "Come on, mi pimienta. The quality of mercy is not strained; It droppeth as the gentle rain from heaven upon the place beneath."

My whole body hummed at the sound of that nickname again. A small squeak escaped my mouth as my lips parted. Okay, Liv had been right. He was *totally* lickable. Why boys didn't spend all of their time memorizing Shakespeare was beyond me.

"What does that mean? Mi pimienta?" I crossed my

fingers behind my back, hoping it didn't have anything to do with picnics.

He smiled. "It's your name. Pimienta is Spanish for Pepper."

He'd called me, *my Pepper.* "Okay, so you speak Spanish and memorized some Shakespeare." I let my gaze drop to my boots. I tried to shrug, to feign indifference, but I was not above the "sceptered sway" of the sexy, self-satisfied smirk he was sporting when his eyes met mine.

"I've had a little time recently." He tipped his head as he stepped closer, his hand still on my shoulder. "Needed something to keep my mind off certain things… and people."

Swallowing, heart in my throat, I nodded.

He cocked an eyebrow. "Guess what else I finished."

I had to take a measured breath to make sure my voice wouldn't be all fluttery. My fuzzy brain managed to latch onto the title in the fugue of my feelings.

"*A Tale of Two Cities*? What did you think?"

He nodded, his dark eyes sparkling. "Lovely and heartbreaking, just like you said."

I let out a little squeal and grabbed his hand, pulling him with me to the nearest table. I plopped down and rested my chin in my hands as I leaned forward.

"Who was your favorite?" I asked. "No, wait—don't answer that. I want to guess."

Alex laughed as I scanned the ceiling in thought.

"Well, there's Sydney—of course."

"Of course." Alex nodded, watching me.

"But Madame Defarge is kind of wonderful in a terrible way." I immediately bunched up my nose, at my own mention of the literary villain.

I had actually been thinking about the idea of villains a lot in the past few days. There was such a big part of me that felt sympathetic toward Stephanie. The woman had looked so broken when she'd found out the truth about the non-existent affair.

My voice sounded thin and small when I finally said, "Stephanie didn't know her mother had started the conversation, she didn't know they'd never gone through with any of it." I shook my head. "She must've found Fergie's letter somehow. Don't you feel kinda bad for her?" I croaked.

Alex reached forward and took my hands in his. "I don't believe anyone's purely bad or purely good. Actually, I agree with you. Some of my favorite characters are flawed and do terrible things. It's what they do in the end that shows their true selves."

I moved my fingers against his, loving the feel of my skin against his. "You really think she'll be okay?"

Alex scoffed. "I wasn't talking about Stephanie. She's literally the worst, Pepper. You remember when she held us at gunpoint, right?"

I laughed, wobbling my head from side to side. I had to give him that.

"No," he said. "I was talking about Madame Defarge. Actually, my mom thought she was really interesting, too." My face must've crumpled in confusion, because after a few silent moments, he added, "She read a lot of classics. Had a list of the ones she'd finished and notes on how she liked it, which characters were her favorite, which scenes she loved or hated. That's why I'm reading through them. Makes me feel closer to her."

It had been a long and emotional few days and Alex's sweet confession about his mother almost brought me to tears.

"She would've liked you." His deep voice folded around me.

He leaned forward across the small two-seater table and reached his hand up to brush gently across my cheek. My eyes locked onto his, then his soft lips met mine, making my eyelids flutter closed and my shoulders relax. I couldn't resist my feelings for Alex any longer and honestly, I didn't want to.

The kiss only lasted for a few glorious seconds, but they were enough to make all of those sappy Shakespeare sonnets suddenly feel totally justified. When he pulled back, his lips were quirked up into a grin and I couldn't help but do the same.

The room was still feeling slightly wobbly, though, and my brain searched for an anchor, something to ground me. That was when I noticed the lamp. Small Dark and Red. We were at my perfect-date table. Everything was perfect.

"I'm sorry." Alex's voice was a little hoarse, which made me feel better. At least I wasn't the only one reeling. "I've been wanting to do that for a while."

"Don't be sorry," I whispered.

But there was a pained expression marring Alex's face and he shook his head. "I am. I shouldn't have done it."

Suddenly it all came back to me: why I didn't want to date guys from college, Michael moving on, everyone leaving me behind. My heart felt like a book cracked right down the spine. *Oh no.* I'd gone and done it all over again.

"You're leaving?"

His jaw tightened as his eyes scanned my face. "Yeah."

I pulled in a deep breath. "Well, that sucks."

Alex chuckled. "No Shakespeare quote for this situation?"

Oh, just about a billion. No one did angst better than The Bard. But at the moment, I didn't feel like quoting anyone, which spoke volumes about my condition.

He sat back, appearing to take my silence as a "no."

"When?" I asked.

"Two and a half weeks."

I felt hope deflate from my body, leaving me a sagging mess. That was even sooner than I'd feared. "But the end of term isn't until December."

"The only classes I'm taking are online and they've got an opening at the academy, so… I have to head south for a few months." He pursed his lips to one side, making the corner of his mouth disappear into an adorable dimple.

"A few months?" I blinked.

His face fell. "I know, it's terrible timing."

My heart hammered in my chest. "No. I mean—you said, 'a few months.' You're coming back?"

"Yeah." He nodded. "The only academy in the state is down by Seattle. It's going to be close to five months, but—" His voice cut out and he rubbed a hand over his face and let out a derisive snort. "It sounds even worse when I say it aloud. Five months is a *long* time."

I had just assumed he'd be leaving like everyone else. But he was planning on coming back! Toes scrunching in the wool socks I'd bunched into my boots this morning, I felt a quote fill my mind like color returning to pale cheeks. "Pleasure and action make the hours seem short."

The sly look on Alex's face made me wrinkle my nose.

"Sorry, I thought that was going to sound less… like an innuendo," I said.

He laughed.

I shook my head. "It's also from *Othello*, which is really not the vibe I think we're going for here." I motioned in between us with my hand.

Alex didn't seem to mind my less than eloquent wording and his grin only widened. Then his hand was slipping behind my neck and he was leaning forward again, letting those sonnet-worthy lips meet mine. I breathed him in and closed my eyes.

It was a kiss worthy of the end of a story. But I hoped it was the beginning of a new one, instead.

Don't miss the next installment of the Pepper Brooks Cozy Mysteries, *Literally Murder*.

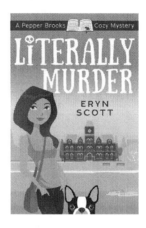

A Farewell to Blondes

When a young woman shows up dead in Campus Creek, amateur sleuth Pepper Brooks is warned not to get involved. She's fine with that. The last thing she needs is to upset her maybe-boyfriend Alex, the newly minted cop.

It's her final quarter of college; she's immersed in Hemingway and planning her future. But when two more fair-haired women show up drowned, Pepper literally can't stay away. Especially when her best friend may be the next one *For Whom the Bell Tolls*.

Get your copy today!

ALSO BY ERYN SCOTT

Mystery:

The Pepper Brooks Cozy Mystery Series

The Stoneybrook Mysteries

Women's fiction:

The Beauty of Perhaps

Settling Up

The What's in a Name Series

In Her Way

Romantic comedy:

Meet Me in the Middle

ABOUT THE AUTHOR

Eryn Scott lives in the Pacific Northwest with her husband and their quirky animals. She loves classic literature, musicals, knitting, and hiking. She writes women's fiction and cozy mysteries.

Join her mailing list to learn about new releases and sales!

www.erynwrites.com
erynwrites@gmail.com